<u>Murder Under A Wolf Moon</u>

A Mona Moon Mystery
Book Five

Abigail Keam

Worker Bee Press

Published in the USA by

Worker Bee Press
P.O. Box 485
Nicholasville, KY 40340

1

"You look crackers tonight, darling," Lord Farley said to Mona as they sped along Versailles Road at twenty-five miles per hour in Mona's chauffeur-driven red and black Daimler. It was dark and the road was slippery with ice.

Mona smiled and answered, "Thank you, Robert. A lady always likes to be complimented, but in America the word 'crackers' has a negative connotation."

Robert replied, "Then you look ravishing. How's that?"

Mona nodded and took a sterling compact out of her purse in order to check her lipstick.

Robert gave Mona the once-over. She was wearing her sleeveless black velvet gown with the sweetheart neckline and elbow-length black gloves. The dress was accented by a long strand of pearls held together by a diamond clip. Her evening coat was a heavy, black brocade as the night was cold due to a winter storm several days before.

Mona glanced over at Robert, approving of his evening tux, black cape, and silver-handled walking stick. He also smelled divine. "You look mighty spiffy yourself."

"Spiffy. That's a new American term for me."

"It means you look okay, bub."

"Darling! You're shivering."

"I'm cold. I think I'm still recovering from our trek to the mountains."

"It was a shame you missed your first Christmas and New Year's Eve in Moon Manor only to be fighting for your life on Pine Mountain."

"I was bored and wanted some adventure," Mona laughed. "That's what I got—only the joke was played on me."

"A little too much adventure."

Mona placed her hand over Robert's. "The only thing I regret is that I put you in danger. I can never forgive myself for doing so. I should have checked out Rupert Hunt more thoroughly.

I'm so sorry, Robert. Really."

"I never liked the man, but I must say his scheme to kidnap you without you knowing it was devilishly clever. He got you to go along with his plan willingly."

"So you forgive me for hiring Rupert later?"

"I guess it takes a thief to catch a thief."

"He's already given Moon Enterprises good information on embezzling in our Butte, Montana office."

"Hiring him is not something I would have done, but things seem to have a way of working out for you, Mona."

"Yes, it's a brand new year and all that trouble is behind us. Roosevelt is fixing the country, and we are heading toward a brighter future."

Robert kissed the inside of Mona's wrist. "And our future as well."

Mona looked deeply into Robert's eyes. "To our future as well," she echoed before shivering again.

"Why aren't you wearing one of your grandmother's fur coats?"

"I hate wearing dead animal skins. It makes me feel—well, uneasy."

Lawrence Robert Emerton Dagobert Farley, Marquess of Gower, had noticed that Mona was slowly weeding her wardrobe of leather and furs. He had thought this new indulgence odd, but had said nothing. Instead, Robert was rather proud of Mona's compassion for animals. Pulling her close, he said, "Let me warm you. It is a chilly night."

Mona snuggled close to him, sighing contentedly.

"I see you are still not wearing my engagement ring."

"I shall wear it when we announce our betrothal and not before."

"Let's do it tonight."

"And spoil the evening for our hostess? I should say not. By the way, who exactly are our host and hostess tonight?"

Robert pulled out a linen paper invitation from his pocket. "Mr. and Mrs. Cornelius Vanderbilt Hopper."

"The Vanderbilt family?"

"A minor cousin with the name but none of the money. Cornelius goes by the name of Connie."

"Did you know that a centurion named Cornelius was directed by an angel to contact St. Peter? After he spoke with Peter, he converted to Christianity and is considered the first gentile convert. Here's another fun fact, Connie means wolf in old German."

"You know the oddest trivia."

Mona shrugged. "I guess I thought of it because there is a wolf moon tonight."

"A what?"

"A full moon in January is called a wolf moon. Don't ask me why. It just is."

Robert peered out of the car window at the sky. "It is a full moon. I didn't even notice. Looks like it's going to snow, too." He leaned back in the seat and put his arm around Mona.

"What else can you tell me about them?" Mona asked.

"The family did have money at one time, but Connie's father was a notorious gambler and frittered all the family's money away."

"Ooh, not good."

"I mean they are not poor by any means, but the family is not Vanderbilt rich anymore. They are just comfortable." Robert thought for a moment. "Well, maybe scratching by. I've heard tales."

"They can't be too poor if they are throwing a big shindig tonight. Champagne costs money."

"Connie is throwing this bash for everyone to meet his new young wife. She has some money, which is why he can afford this bash."

"Go on."

"Her name is Elspeth Neferet Alden. Her father was Sir Jonathon Alden."

"The famous Egyptologist?"

"I knew that would impress you."

"Oh, my goodness. I can't wait to meet her and talk about her father's exploits."

Robert was delighted when Mona's yellow eyes lit up with excitement. She liked nothing better than to discuss the ancient world in the Near East. It was her passion.

The Daimler pulled up in front of a beige limestone mansion with its windows blazing with light as though a thousand candles had been lit. Jamison, Mona's chauffeur, opened the car door.

Robert jumped out first and gave a hand to Mona, who stared at the mansion.

Mona commented, "This is bigger than Moon

Mansion. Must cost a fortune for the upkeep."

"Now you see the need for this marriage."

"Oh," was all Mona could utter before the door was opened by the butler and Mona was whisked out of the cold.

2

Mona handed her wrap to a maid and then let Robert escort her into the ballroom. A live orchestra was playing the latest popular radio tunes, and the floor was alive with guests dancing the foxtrot, while older couples danced the black bottom and Charleston.

Robert and Mona stood in the receiving line and waited their turn to greet their hosts. Finally, Mona was presented to Cornelius Vanderbilt Hopper.

"It's a pleasure meeting you," Cornelius said. He kissed Mona's hand. "Everything they say about you is true. You are a beauty like the rarest orchid."

"Not half of what *they* say about me is accurate Mr. Hopper," Mona replied. She didn't know what to make of Hopper's flamboyant comments.

"I thought people were exaggerating about your hair, but it is truly platinum, without any benefit of color—and your eyes—a true yellow, more of a golden hue I would think."

Annoyed, Robert stepped in and held out his hand. "Good to see you again, Connie."

Shaking his hand, Hopper said, "Robert, how nice to see you. Are you here with this gorgeous creature?"

"Yes, I am, so mittens off."

"Speaking of gorgeous creatures, may I present my wife, Elspeth Neferet Alden Hopper."

Both Robert and Mona turned to the petite, dusky-skinned, dark-haired woman with black soulful eyes standing beside Hopper. Robert gave a little bow, but Mona was so smitten with admiration that she could barely find words to speak.

Mrs. Hopper was wearing a pleated, linen sheath adorned with a large Egyptian collar called a wesekh made of gold, turquoise, coral, onyx, and lapis lazuli. The woman's dark eyes were outlined in kohl like the ancient Egyptians. The only difference in her makeup from that of an ancient woman was that Mrs. Hopper wore bright red lipstick.

For a second, Mona thought she was addressing Nefertiti. "Em hotep."

Mrs. Hopper became animated and said, "Ii-wey. You speak ancient Egyptian?"

"Just a few lines I picked up when I was in Cairo. I am more familiar with Sumerian and Babylonian words. I must say I am so taken with your collar. It looks authentic."

"My father made it from bits and pieces he found in the sand. He presented it to me on my eighteenth birthday."

"Lucky girl," Mona said, barely taking her eyes off the collar. Jewelry was a weakness of Mona's.

"My dear, people are waiting," Connie said to Elspeth.

"You're right, Connie. Forgive me. Miss Moon, I hope we have a chance to speak again this evening."

Mona said, "Please, we must. I am dying to talk about the Near East and your adventures excavating Queen Ahsetsedek's tomb."

Elspeth asked, "You know of my father's work?"

"Who doesn't know about John Alden and his famous find in the Valley of the Queens?" Mona said.

"Dear!" Connie said as though annoyed.

For a second, Elspeth's eyes dampened but she nodded and smiled.

Robert led Mona over to a chair. "Happy?"

"I'm ecstatic, Robert. I'm so glad you made me come. Think of it—John Alden's daughter. Oh, the stories she must have. I can't wait to get her alone."

"Are you up for a dance while you're waiting?"

"Assuredly."

Robert led Mona onto the dance floor where they did the foxtrot, a waltz, and another foxtrot until Mona begged off.

"It's hot in this room, that's for sure," Robert said.

"I need to freshen up. Can you excuse me?"

"Don't take too long. I see some captains of industry heading my way for some boring shop talk."

"I promise."

Mona gathered her clutch from the coat check

maid and headed for the downstairs bathroom for the ladies, but it was too crowded, so she asked if she could use the upstairs one. The maid pointed to a powder room on the second floor. Mona quickly bounded up the grand staircase and headed down a carpeted hallway. Passing one of the doors cracked open, she heard crying—a deep mournful crying. Standing at the door, Mona looked both ways, wondering what she should do. No one else was in the hallway. Crying was a private act and Mona didn't want to intrude, but crying also meant someone might need help. She knocked on the door and peeked in. Inside a spacious and luxurious bedroom, Elspeth sat on a chair holding her magnificent necklace.

"Elspeth, what is the matter?" Mona quickly closed the door, locked it, and went to the weeping bride.

"You shouldn't be in here."

"You shouldn't be crying at your own party." Mona dragged a chair close to Elspeth. "Now tell me. What is the matter?"

"Connie told me to change into something more conservative. He said my dress embarrassed him and looked like something a person would wear at Halloween."

"You looked stunning. I love the collar. In fact, I have half a mind to steal it," Mona teased.

Elspeth looked at Mona through thick, tear-stained eyelashes. "I wore it to honor my father. Did you really like my outfit?"

"My dear, your dress was fascinating and quite wonderful. Who cares what Connie says?"

"I don't want to make my husband angry."

"Okay, change then, but no more tears. Don't let those people downstairs see you cry, and when you go back down, tell everyone you tore the hem of your linen dress while dancing." Mona went over to a wall, which was lined with mirrors. "Is this your closet?"

Elspeth nodded.

Mona threw open all the mirrored doors to Elspeth's wardrobe. "Let's find the most seductive gown you have."

"Connie wants me to wear something conservative."

"Listen, my dear, if you give in to ridiculous demands now, your husband won't give you a moment's peace. You will never be your own woman. Understand?"

Elspeth wiped away a tear. "It's true what they say about you."

"What's that?" Mona asked, rummaging through the closet.

"That you are different. A leopard among house cats."

"Do they? That's rather nice, don't you think? I like leopards. I recently had a bout with a mountain panther."

"Who won?"

Mona laughed. "It was a draw." She pulled a low-cut red chiffon dress from the closet. "This will do nicely. Wear this."

"Oh, no. I can't. It's too risqué."

"You'll wear it or you'll be under your husband's thumb the rest of your life. Now, we need some jewelry. Do you have a necklace to set off that dress?"

"I have a diamond choker."

"Do you have something that will plunge into your cleavage?"

Elspeth's hands fluttered a bit. "I have a ruby and diamond pin that can change into a necklace."

"Sounds perfect." Mona threw the dress at Elspeth. "Put it on." She went over to Elspeth's vanity and rummaged through her jewelry box finding the pin and then a heavy chain for it. Mona clasped the necklace around Elspeth neck. "Looks lovely. Now we need to fix your makeup." Mona dusted Elspeth's face with powder and redid her lipstick with a brighter shade of red.

"I hope Connie likes this dress."

"He probably won't. He'll make a fuss after the party."

"I don't want that."

"It doesn't matter what dress you select. He will deem it inappropriate. Don't you understand?"

"What do you mean?"

Mona looked Elspeth directly in the eyes. "You know exactly what I mean." She grabbed one of Elspeth's arms. "Where did you get that bruise?"

Elspeth pulled her arm away. "I fell."

"Sure you did."

"It was an accident."

"Sure it was."

Elspeth looked away. "I have no friends or family here. It's terribly frightening being alone in a strange place without anyone to talk with."

"Then you must come to tea tomorrow at Moon Manor. I know what it is like to be alone in new surroundings. Tell Connie I'm having a hen party so you can meet more ladies in the community. Will you come?"

"That's awfully sweet of you, but you needn't bother with me. We don't know each other and—I don't want to be a nuisance."

"I have tea at four o'clock. Be there."

"Will you walk down with me? I don't want to face Connie in this dress alone."

"Of course. I need to use the powder room first though. Nature calls." Mona strode off to the bathroom and after refreshing herself, checking her outfit, and putting on more lipstick, she entered Elspeth's bedroom only to find her gone.

"She left without me," Mona said to herself. She hurried to the grand staircase where she discovered Connie berating Elspeth on the stair landing. Elspeth was looking down at her feet and anxiously twisting a handkerchief between two sweaty palms.

"My goodness," Mona called out from above. "You've changed into another dress, Elspeth." She hurried down the steps and twirled Elspeth around. "It's a stunner, dear. Don't you think so, Mr. Hopper, I mean, Connie?" Mona didn't give him time to answer. "Come on, Elspeth. You'll simply bowl people over. I know a lot of women here tonight who will want a gander at your necklace. Ruby, isn't it? From India? Two stunning necklaces in one night. You put us all to shame."

Mona turned to Connie. "You must be so proud. Your wife is surely going to be the social butterfly of the season. Come Elspeth. You must show this dress off. Will you excuse us, Connie— or would you like the honor of escorting your wife?"

Connie's face flushed red and was so overcome with anger, he couldn't sputter any reply to Mona, nor would he have if he could have found the words. He realized she was toying with him, so all he could do was to take his wife's arm and guide her down the stairs into the ballroom. Connie wouldn't dare offend Mona, as she was too powerful.

"Don't forget tea tomorrow at four, Elspeth. Ladies only. I insist," Mona called after her. Smiling, Mona glided down the staircase into the arms of Robert.

Robert asked, "Why do you look so pleased with yourself?"

"I just bullied a bully."

"Really?"

"Yes, really."

"Tell me about it in the car. Ready to skip this popsicle stand?"

"Most assuredly."

"I'll grab our coats. You say goodbye to our hosts."

Mona shook her head. "I really think we can forget that part of the evening."

Robert laughed. "What did you do, darling?"

"I'll tell you about it at your house in front of a roaring fire with hot chocolate."

"Will you stay the night?"

"And give the servants something to gossip about? No way, but I might be convinced to see the wolf moon sink behind the horizon."

"I'll take what I can get." Robert rushed off to gather their coats. With the promise of a little snogging, Robert couldn't wait to get Mona to his house. And there was Mona's encounter. Robert could only guess what had occurred.

Hmm—what could Mona possibly have instigated now?

3

Robert was nibbling Mona's earlobe.

"What can you tell me about Connie Hopper?" she asked.

"How can you think about Connie when I'm doing this?" Robert nuzzled Mona's neck.

"Feels lovely."

"More the response I was hoping for, woman. Now turn around so I can give you a proper snog. Let's swap some saliva."

After kissing for a while, Mona came up for air. "How well do you know Hopper?"

"You still thinking about that man? If you are going to think about another man while I'm trying to seduce you, what chance do we have?"

"Don't sulk, Robert. You know how my mind works. There's a puzzle concerning Espeth and

Connie. My mind can't turn off. It keeps racing."

Robert reached for a cigarette and lit it.

"I wish you wouldn't smoke, Robert."

"I smoke out of frustration, Mona. It's due to you."

"The sooner you tell me the sooner we can get back to necking."

"Oh, well, then." Robert stubbed out his cigarette and took a sip of his coffee while Mona took a drink of her hot chocolate spiked with a touch of liqueur. He didn't know how she could stand the combination. Robert did know that he couldn't touch liquor for a year in order to get Mona to marry him. He also knew Mona deliberately tempted him by drinking alcohol in front of him. She was a devil. "I don't know him very well. He's quite a bit older than I. We're not in business or anything like that."

"How do you know him?"

"I guess the Bluegrass social circuit. Love of horse racing, that sort of thing."

"What do people say about him?"

Robert shrugged. "Not much, I'm afraid. Connie's always been very low key. No scandals of any sort. He has reasonably good manners.

Knows which fork to use at a dinner party and never discusses politics or religion with anyone. Never gossips about anyone. Never been seen in the female servants' quarters after midnight. He's one dull boy if you ask me."

"Unlike you."

"Definitely unlike me."

"Hmm."

"Why this interest in Connie Hopper? Did he do something to you? Shall I fight him in a duel at dawn?"

"I was just wondering."

"Wondering what?"

"Why a young woman like Elspeth, who is British and has her own money, would marry a much older man who is American and basically broke?"

"You once called the British snobs of the worst kind."

"I did?"

"Yes, you did and you're quite right. Elspeth doesn't have the right breeding credentials for a brilliant upper class British marriage."

Mona looked flummoxed. "She's John Alden's daughter, the greatest Egyptologist who ever lived. He discovered Queen Ahsetsedek IV's tomb intact."

"John Alden was born in an East London slum from an unmarried working girl, if you know what I mean."

"I see where this is going. I guess it doesn't matter that Alden elevated himself from the 'gutter' and worked his way to a Ph.D. from Oxford."

"I never mentioned the word gutter."

"But that's what you meant."

"I'm trying to tell you why Elspeth married whom she did if you let me finish."

"Sorry."

"John Alden was a cockney who went on to achieve many wonderful things, but then he marries an Egyptian native, which resulted in Elspeth."

"I see what you're saying. The noses of the blue bloods across the pond were bent out of shape, and they wouldn't let Elspeth play with their sons."

"Exactly. Both classism and racism played into the scenario."

"Well, boy of mine. What are *they* going to say

about me when we marry?"

"My British *friends* are going to insult you behind your back, but they will be polite to your
face. You're too rich for them to offend, and they
can't afford to be rude because they figure that in
twenty years they'll palm one of their worthless
offspring onto one of our offspring. That's the
way it will be."

"Why should I marry you?"

"Because you love me and no matter what, we
are going to do what we want to do—similar to
what your parents did. They crossed social lines
to be married, didn't they?"

"Oh, how can I refuse you, Robert, when you
make such sense? Yes, my father lost the Moon
inheritance because he married my mother."

"Were they happy, Babycakes?"

"They loved each other very much. It hurt my
father to lose his inheritance, but he loved my
mother too much to let her go. Yes, Robert, they
were fortunate because they realized money can't
bring happiness. Love does."

"Money can sure keep wolves away from the
door, though," Robert teased. On a more serious
note, he said, "We'll be okay, Mona. Trust me.

No one will ever hurt you if I can help it."

"Promise?"

Robert took his index finger and crossed his heart. "Hope to die."

Mona snuggled closer to Robert on the couch. "We'll be happy, won't we?"

"No one will touch us," Robert promised.

Little did Robert know when he uttered those words that he would be proven wrong.

Trouble was fast approaching.

4

"It's so nice of you to have me," Elspeth said to Mona after Samuel showed her into the drawing room. She was wearing a hunter-green suit accented by wide lapels and a white silk blouse. The skirt was flared and fell just below the knees. The suit's belt was brown as were Elspeth's shoes, gloves, and purse. A jaunty green felt hat with several pheasant feathers perched on her upswept hairdo.

Mona couldn't help but notice there was a run in one of Elspeth's stockings and what appeared to be cat hair on her jacket. "I'm glad you could come."

Elspeth glanced about the white-painted room with its modern furniture and marble floors. "This room is so bright and cheerful. I wish I could redo Connie's home. The furniture is so dark and cumbersome looking. Very Victorian. It's quite depressing."

"I know what you mean. We had a fire last year, which gave me the opportunity to redo the house. Of course, at the time I was devastated, but I've added an elevator, the servants' quarters were updated, all the bathrooms were enlarged and modernized as were the plumbing and electrical wiring. The place was pretty much gutted."

"Connie said it was your housekeeper who set Moon Manor on fire."

"He's correct. She set it on fire with me in it. Well, that's in the past. Let's not dwell upon it. Please have a seat. I'm sorry Samuel didn't collect your coat."

"I told him I'd rather keep it myself." She placed her brown and white houndstooth, wool coat beside her before taking off her gloves and putting them in her purse. "No one else coming?"

"I thought it would be nice if we could chat alone."

"Thank you. A room full of people makes me

nervous. I guess you could say I'm the bashful type. Nervous Nellie—that's what Connie calls me."

"How charming," Mona replied, sarcastically.

Elspeth bit her lip and wiped her mouth smearing her lipstick.

Mona handed her a linen napkin. "Your lipstick needs a touch-up, dear."

Elspeth reached for her purse and pulled out a compact. Dismayed at her reflection, she blurted, "See, what I mean. I can't even wear lipstick without smudging my face."

"Every woman sullies her lipstick," Mona said. "No need for concern."

"Look! Now, I've got it on your lovely napkin. Oh, I'm such a mess," Elspeth said, bursting into tears.

Mona studied Elspeth for a moment and then rose and poured a glass of bourbon before pulling the servant's cord. "Here. Try this. It will help settle your nerves."

Elspeth sniffed the glass and took a small sip and then another.

Samuel knocked on the door and entered. "Yes, Miss Mona?"

"Tell cook to ready the dishes I requested."

"Shall I remove the tea service?"

"No, we'll start with the tea repast and then work our way through the other courses."

Samuel stole a quick look at Elspeth before departing.

Elspeth wiped her eyes. "You can see why Connie despises me. I'm such a ninny."

"Why would you marry a man who despises you?" Mona asked while pouring tea. "Milk? Sugar?"

"Milk, please," Elspeth said, taking a deep breath and reaching for the teacup.

"Angel food cake?"

"I'm not a big fan of sweets."

"I am," Mona said, piling slices of angel food and fruit cake on her plate. "The watercress sandwiches are tasty as are the egg salad ones."

Elspeth took several small sandwiches. "I don't know how you keep your lovely figure eating angel food cake."

"You didn't answer my question."

"You didn't answer mine."

Mona laughed. "All right, I'll go first. I'm up at dawn and don't stop until I go to bed. I eat a large breakfast, have only a sandwich or salad for lunch, and then splurge at tea time. I'm afraid it's a vice with me. I don't drink much or smoke, but I do love my tea sandwiches and cakes in the afternoon."

Samuel reentered the room with a serving cart. He pushed the cart near Mona. "Shall I serve?"

"Yes, please. I think our guest would like some hummus with the pita bread and the tomato and cucumber salad."

"Hummus in the middle of the Bluegrass!" Elspeth looked astounded. "A taste of home. Where in the world did you get pita bread?"

"My cook is a wizard. After all, pita bread is just leavened flatbread. Simple enough to make and hummus is nothing more than chickpeas, which are grown in California."

Samuel handed Elspeth a plate.

She tasted the hummus and moaned. "This is so good. Tastes like it's from a café in Cairo. A little more lemon I think, though."

"I will advise the cook," Samuel said.

Elspeth gave a faint smile as she watched Samuel leave the room. "I wish my servants were as efficient as yours. I've had nothing but trouble with my staff."

"My rule is simple. I pay very well for that efficiency. If an employee doesn't meet my standards, he is let go. That is understood working for Moon Enterprises."

"Everyone seems content working here. Moon Manor has a calmness about it. There's always tension at my home with the staff."

Mona didn't reply as she took a sip of her tea.

"You seem very satisfied with your life, Mona. I wish I could say the same. You asked why I married Connie Hopper. Don't feel sorry for me. I knew what I was getting into. I knew he didn't love me."

"But you're John Alden's daughter. You could have had your pick."

"There's the rub. I had plenty of men wanting to sleep with me, but none wanted to marry me. It's my Egyptian blood to which the so-called suitors objected. I am financially independent, but I want children, you see. Very much, so I needed to be married."

"So Connie came along."

"I met him at an embassy party in London.

He was older and seemed settled. His first wife had died and his only son was grown. He was not averse to starting a new family. Here's the funny thing. Connie didn't even know who my father was."

"Did he know you were rich?"

Elspeth nodded. "I'm a practical person. We can't all have a love match. Sometimes women have to make compromises. Connie was up front with me. He said he wasn't wealthy anymore, but that he would be a good husband and father, giving me the children I want."

"I see."

"I had Connie investigated by a private detective. No scandals in his background except for his father gambling away the Hopper fortune. We were two lonely people who needed each other. He needed money and I needed a husband."

"How is the marriage working out?"

"I don't want to seem disloyal, but Connie is a terrible scold. Everything I do is wrong. He makes me so nervous sometimes that I think I'll scream."

"What about the bruise on your arm?"

"We were arguing on the staircase landing,

and I took a step back, almost tumbling down the stairs. Connie grabbed me. He was trying to save me from harm, not hurt me."

Mona felt that Elspeth was telling the truth. She didn't feel so hostile toward Connie now. "What were you two arguing about?"

"Connie wants control over my father's antiquities."

"For what purpose?"

"I think he wants to sell the collection."

"Is he having money issues?"

"I have enough money for all our needs, but he seems obsessed with my father's treasure. What I have left at the end of my life is for our children's inheritance. Case closed as far as I'm concerned."

"What did Connie say about the red dress?"

"Surprisingly, nothing."

"I think Connie might be all about appearances. If others complimented you on your change of evening gown, he would have been satisfied."

"Perhaps. I kept waiting for Connie to say something this morning, but he was quiet on the subject except that he thought the reception went well."

Mona raised an eyebrow.

"I realize we don't know each other terribly well, but I feel I can trust you. I understand that you are a woman of considerable boldness—a modern woman who does not depend upon a man to help her wend her way in the world."

"Well, I don't know about that," Mona said.

Elspeth held up her hand. "My father was at an advanced age when I was born. He was of the Victorian mind that children should be seen—not heard. My mother was a typical woman from her culture. She was taught to obey her husband in all things. So, you see, I am struggling to be a woman living in the United States where women can vote and do things without their husband's permission—a modern woman. I want to learn to be an American woman like you."

"That's very flattering, but being like me will cause conflict in your marriage. I'm a little bold in my thinking."

"I don't want my marriage to fail, but I don't like being told what to do or how to think by a man who never bothers to understand my point of view. I had enough of that with my father." Elspeth waved her hand in frustration. "Connie is not a bad man. He is very insecure, though. He feels his lack of money makes others consider him a failure, and in many ways, he is correct. Connie was never able to build his family's fortune back to where it had been."

"How could he in this Depression? How could anyone?"

"You have. I understand your mines are going to have a record year."

"That is due to the efforts of many people besides myself. I have a great team working for me." Mona put down her cup.

"There is something I must do before I begin my transformation into a more contemporary woman."

"What's that?"

"Stay alive."

5

"Pardon?" Mona said, thinking she had not heard correctly.

"Someone has been threatening to kill me." Elspeth pulled several pieces of paper from her purse and handed them to Mona. They were three pages torn from a child's notebook tablet with individual letters cut from magazines and crudely pasted to form threatening messages.

Mona used her handkerchief to hold them.

"Have you had these tested for fingerprints?"

"Yes. Nothing."

"Hmm," Mona said while studying the notes. "Were they creased like this when you got them?"

"They were folded with two crease lines. The other creases were caused by me hiding them in my purse."

"What type of envelope?"

"Business."

She sniffed the letters. "This one smells faintly of tobacco smoke."

"I noticed that as well."

"*You will die,*" Mona read out loud, matter-of-factly. "This one is cute—*you have only a few days to live.* And for the last one—*your mother was a whore.* Typical threats made to a woman—warnings of violence and sexual shaming."

"Are you saying I shouldn't take these threats seriously?"

"On the contrary, I think you should take them very seriously."

"Oh."

"How were they delivered?"

"Though the mail."

"Where are the envelopes?"

"I threw them away."

"Stamps?"

"Nothing unusual."

"If you get another one, keep the envelope."

Elspeth nodded and looked hopefully at Mona.

"Do you remember the postmarks?"

"One was from London, one was from New York, and the last one was from Cincinnati."

"Can you show me the order in which you received them?"

"The one about my mother was first, the second one was about my demise, and the third one was about my having a few days left."

"And you say they came in the post?"

"Yes," Elspeth replied, wiping perspiration off her upper lip.

"Were the letters opened when given to you?"

"No. They were sealed shut."

"Do you think they had been tampered with?"

"I don't understand."

"Sometimes nosey maids or housekeepers use steam to open their employer's mail."

"I don't think that is the case. The mail is usually given to me directly after it is delivered."

"By whom?"

"My maid, Beulah. She's been with me for years. I hired her when my mother was dying. She has helped me a great deal throughout the years."

"You pay her well?"

"The standard scale."

"You might want to rethink that. The 'standard' pay wouldn't keep a poor church mouse in cheese these days."

"Are you saying Beulah is responsible?"

"I'm saying you need to pay your staff better. A good wage cuts through many petty resentments by the employee in the employer/employee relationship. Just a piece of advice. I've been on both sides of that equation, and people like to be appreciated for their work." Mona returned to the letters and thought for a moment. "When did you receive these letters?"

"I got the first one in London right after I married Connie. The other two after I arrived here."

"Ever received anything like these before?"

"When one lives in England and has a parent of non-British descent, all sorts of nasty things are implied, especially from the cream of British society."

"The Brits are terrible snobs, aren't they? The sun never sets on their Empire and all that tommyrot. Getting back to the letters, you think these are different?"

"I've never received one with cut-out magazine letters which portend my death. Usually, threats are typed or written in longhand saying *go home* or *you don't belong here*—things like that. These have a different feel to me. For the first time, I'm frightened."

"Were the addresses on the envelopes written or typed?"

"Typed."

"Return address?"

"Each one was different."

"I wish we had those addresses."

"I wrote them down and had them checked out. Each one was bogus."

"So, you have done some work on these letters?"

"As much as I dared."

"I see. I think it odd that two of these notes are in English and the third one is in French. Do you speak French?"

"Yes, along with Arabic."

Mona said, "And ancient Egyptian."

Elspeth returned a small smile. "I can also read and write ancient Greek, Latin, and a smattering of Aramaic."

"With your background and education, why is it you are not carrying on your father's work?"

"What do you mean?"

"I would think you'd want to be another Lady Hester Stanhope. Your name alone can open many doors."

Elspeth said, "I have started a project. I have been communicating with the director of the Cincinnati Art Museum about having an exhibit of my father's artifacts. We are working on the details. If that exhibit is successful, I plan to take it to Chicago."

Mona clapped her hands in delight. "That is wonderful. Now everyone will be able to see your father's work and Queen Ahsetsedek's tomb relics. I take it that her gold funeral mask will be exhibited as well?"

Elspeth nodded. "There is something else, too, of which my husband is not aware."

"What?"

"I plan to write a biography of my father. I've typed up his handwritten field notes, and I possess all the original glass negatives of the expedition. You could say I am a leading authority on Queen Ahsetsedek, but what I truly want to do is to restore my father's reputation from that of a treasure hunter like Heinrich Schliemann to that of Howard Carter's international renown."

"The fact that you are going to share your father's work with the world will give much credit to both you and your father."

"Not everyone adores my father as you do. His major work was before the British enforced the antiquity laws. He is considered a grave plunderer by many."

"He's another Arthur Evans."

"He also became rich from the booty he took out of Egypt. The British Museum bought most of the artifacts. I own the rest."

"Do you think these notes have anything to do with that?"

"Possibly. The wesekh I wore at my reception is actually Queen Ahsetsedek's. I tell that story about my father putting it together from bits found in the desert so it will not be considered valuable and snatched off my neck. I hope you will honor this information as confidential."

"I will as I am very familiar with the smuggling trade from my time in Iraq. These men are not to be trifled with. I would also venture a guess that several governments would be interested in what you still possess."

"You see my predicament."

"I do, but I don't see how I can assist you. My dear, anyone could have sent you those letters—your husband, international thieves, or colleagues jealous of your father's success. It boggles the mind."

Elspeth grabbed Mona's hand. "You must help me, Mona. There is no one else I can turn to. I know this is not your problem, but you are a woman of keen intelligence and familiar with danger. You know my world, and you're not afraid of violence."

"I don't go looking for it either."

"Please help me. There is no one else."

Mona grabbed a pencil by the telephone and wrote on a pad. "Do you have any black house staff?"

"The kitchen staff is black."

"Then contact this man and bring him on as an employee. House servants are prolific gossips. If there is anything to find that is nefarious within your home, this man will ferret it out. He is a very capable private investigator."

Elspeth looked at the name. "Jellybean Martin. How shall I contact him?"

"Tell your cook that you wish to speak to Jellybean on a private matter. No one else is to know. She'll get word to him. He'll show up and no one in your family will be the wiser. He is very discreet."

"You think this man can help me?"

"I think he's a start, but you will need overseas contacts as well. Contact my man, Dexter Deatherage. He can recommend a European detective."

"He will keep my secret?"

"Yes, Dexter is a good man. I don't know what I'd do without him." Mona placed her hand on Elspeth's. "This might cost a great deal."

"I will do as you suggest."

Mona winked. "Thatta girl. Grab this situation by the tail and give it a good tug."

Elspeth stood. "Thank you, Mona Moon. I feel we might become very good friends."

"Who says we aren't now?"

Elspeth smiled and took her leave.

Mona stood in the doorway of Moon Manor and watched Elspeth ride away in a silver Rolls Royce, all the time wondering if Elspeth had fabricated those letters herself.

6

"Listen to reason, Mona. I can't tell you anything that was said between Mrs. Hopper and myself. It's privileged."

"What are you—a priest?" Mona snapped back.

Dexter made a face before taking a sip of his coffee.

"You work for me, you know."

"If Mrs. Hopper retains my services, then she is my client as well. Now don't badger me."

"But you are supposed to work for me exclusively."

"Then you shouldn't have recommended me to her."

"Darn," Mona said, exasperated. "You are such a boy scout."

"And if I told you anything she said, you would fire me."

"True."

Dexter laughed. "Quit badgering me then."

Dexter's wife, Willie, spoke up. "I can gossip, Mona. I'm not sworn to protect Dexter's clients."

"My dear! You shock me," Dexter said.

She pulled a cigar out from Dexter's coat pocket. "Smoke this and stow it."

"The only reason Mona invited us for cocktails is to pump information out of us," Dexter said, lighting up his cigar.

"The same as I would do," Willie said, inching forward on the couch with her eyes opened wide with anticipation. "Ask away, Mona."

"It's so nice to be friends with someone who has less scruples than I."

"Mona, you say the most shocking things," Dexter complained.

Willie pooh-poohed her husband. "Mona's only pulling your leg, dear."

"Tell me everything you know about Cornelius Hopper," Mona said.

Willie answered in a voice dripping with affectation. "You mean the Hopper branch of the

Vanderbilt family?"

Mona grinned. "I take it that Connie puts it on pretty thick about his Vanderbilt connection."

"Like ticks on a junkyard dog. He is such a bore at times."

"How long have you known him, Willie?"

Willie looked at her husband for confirmation. "Forever. I went to high school with him. He's two years older."

"Is he an only child?"

"No, he has a sister who lives overseas. Hasn't been back over here in twenty years. I don't know if I would recognize her if I walked past her."

Dexter said, "I think you would, my dear."

Mona asked, "Good student at school?"

"He wasn't a straight A student like I was, but made fairly good grades. I'd say in the top ten percent of his graduating class."

"College?"

"He went to Yale and dropped out in his third year. He wanted to become a doctor."

"Couldn't make it?"

"Oh, no, Mona. His father lost a great deal of money, so Connie had to leave school. You know

I don't think he ever forgave his father."

"What happened then?"

"Connie married Hedda Brugal, who was an heiress. Her father owned rubber plantations."

"This man seems to marry women with considerable bank accounts," Mona said.

"It may have been that in the beginning, but those two grew to love each other deeply. Connie was devoted to Hedda and devastated when she passed away."

"How long were they married?"

"Eight years I think it was," Dexter answered.

"That's about right," Willie concurred.

"How did she die?"

"It was an accident. Hedda fell off a ladder decorating the Christmas tree and hit her head, never to regain consciousness. She died two weeks later."

"Did Connie inherit the rubber plantations?"

"Their son, Cadwallader, did," Willie said, freshening her coffee with cream. "He's called Wally for short."

"Where is he?"

"Wally pops in every now and then. He breeds Thoroughbreds on his father's farm."

"Where does he usually live?"

Willie looked askance at Dexter. "We don't know. If asked, Wally says he moves around a lot."

Dexter scoffed, "He tells people he's a citizen of the universe."

"Interesting," Mona remarked. "If Cadwallader inherited the rubber business, why is his father marrying for money again?"

Willie said, "Wally gives his father a yearly stipend to run the farm and living expenses. Anything over that is Connie's problem. Connie did build his fortune back up prior to his wife's death, but invested in pyramid schemes. When the stock market crashed in 1929, so did he."

Mona said, "Poor Connie. He has the worst luck. I kinda feel for him. No one could have predicted that this depression would have lasted as long as it has. Didn't President Hoover believe it would be over in three weeks?"

Dexter fiddled with his watch fob. He didn't like to talk ill of an American president, but thought Herbert Hoover had been a fool and helped worsen the catastrophe with his lack of federal relief policies.

ABIGAIL KEAM

Mona asked, "Has anyone shown up in town that, how do I say this, looks out of place?"

Dexter said, "If you mean anyone speaking Arabic, then no. Are you expecting visitors from Egypt?"

"Elspeth did tell you about the letters, then," Mona said.

"I can't reveal what a client said, but you told me about the letters when you rang to tell me to expect Elspeth Hopper's call. In fact, you went into great detail about them."

"Did she bring them when she came for her appointment?"

"Mona, I can't say."

"What letters?" Willie asked, looking between Dexter and Mona.

Mona said, "Someone has been sending Elspeth threatening letters. She asked for my help with them."

Willie said, "Better watch it there, Mona. No good deed goes unpunished."

"Keep this to yourself, Willie."

"My lips are sealed."

"I think we should change the subject," Dexter suggested.

"I need to bounce some ideas off you two."

"I'm game," Willie said, excitedly.

"Very well, but only if it is hypothetically," Dexter said, now curious at to why Mona insisted on discussing Elspeth Hopper.

"What do you think is occurring with Mrs. Hopper?" Willie asked of Mona.

"I don't think Elspeth is telling us the entire story."

"How so?" Dexter asked, after taking a long pull on his cigar. He lofted smoke rings toward the ceiling.

"I think she knows who is sending those letters."

"But why come to you then?" Willie asked, waving smoke away from her face.

Mona shook her head. "Perhaps she knows of my work in Iraq. I do have some credible standing in my field of cartography among archeologists."

Dexter said, "Okay, she's heard of you. So what's your beef with her story?"

"Well, for one thing, Elspeth said she wrote down the return addresses of the letters and then threw the envelopes away. That doesn't make sense to me. She's savvy enough to have hired a private investigator to check up on Connie but discards the envelopes. The logical thing is to keep them. She knew a great deal of information could have been gleaned from them."

"Maybe odd behavior, but hardly criminal, Mona," Dexter said.

"Here are the facts as we know them. The letters started arriving after her marriage to Connie. She received one in London, then two here, one from New York, and the other postmarked Cincinnati—basically the route she traveled to get here. One is written in French and the other two in English—all three with cut-out magazine letters. One smells of tobacco smoke."

"What's your point?" Dexter asked.

"We have only Elspeth's word that this happened as she says."

"You think she's lying?" Willie asked.

Mona stirred her coffee. "Here are the possibilities. Elspeth wrote the letters to encourage her husband's sympathy. I don't think their marriage is a great success, and this might be Elspeth's way of giving the marriage a boost. Nothing like a husband saving a damsel from distress."

"I can see that," Dexter said. "I've seen crazier things from wives toward their husbands."

Willie narrowed her eyes. "Oh, really?"

Mona continued, "Then let's say she didn't concoct the letters. The next ring of logical suspects would be Connie, Beulah the maid, or the son, Cadwallader."

"For what purpose?" Dexter asked.

"Personal. Connie wants to make his wife seem unstable to his associates because of a nefarious intent. The maid is peeved about her employment and wants to make her mistress suffer. The stepson resents his father remarrying."

"Given," Dexter said, stubbing out his cigar. "What else?"

"Let's say it's political. The Egyptian government is putting pressure on Elspeth because they want their treasure back, so they are making life unpleasant until she relents."

Dexter said, "I hardly think Sultan Fuad of Egypt would stoop to send threatening letters to a young woman of international repute. He's much more diplomatic than that."

"But he might send agents."

"Far-fetched."

Willie added, "If we are bringing the world stage into this, it could be the work of some fringe Arab nationalist group."

"I've thought of that. Dexter, you have some contacts with the British government. Give them a ring."

Dexter answered, "Already done so, Mona. Nothing stirring in the breeze where that's concerned. The Egyptians are mostly haranguing the Brits about what's in the British Museum. They also want what Napoleon stole from them in 1798. I don't think I can blame them. What if the United States was invaded and our treasures looted by a foreign power? We would be outraged."

"Do we know what Elspeth still has in her possession?" Willie asked, changing the subject.

"That's a good question, Willie. Do we know the contents of her inventory and what it's worth?" Mona said, looking at Dexter.

He took a sip of his coffee and raised his eyebrows.

"I know. I know. You can't talk about it," Mona said, laughing.

"All I can say is that Elspeth Hopper is very well set financially, and her future children will be also."

"Is she as rich as Mona?" Willie asked.

"No, but then who is?"

Mona blushed. She had not grown accustomed to her wealth, and it sometimes embarrassed her. She still considered herself a normal working cartographer.

Noticing Mona's discomfort, Willie said, "Sorry, darling. I know it's uncouth of me to say such things."

Mona started to reply when Lord Farley strode into the room unannounced.

He stopped and sniffed. "Is that cigar smoke I smell?"

"I just had one," Dexter said. "Would you care for a cigar, Robert? I have them custom made in Havanna."

Robert gave Mona a sour look. "Mona lets you smoke a cigar in Moon Manor but I am forbidden to sneak one wee cigarette."

"I'm not marrying Dexter. I need you in fit condition," Mona said, as she poured coffee for Robert.

Willie clapped her hands together. "So you two are getting hitched? When's the blessed day?"

"We are unofficially engaged," Robert pouted, putting the coffee cup on a side table.

"I hope you both keep this under your hat," Mona said.

"Are you engaged, Mona Moon, or are you not?" Willie demanded.

Robert sat on the arm of Mona's chair and leaned close to her. "Are we, dearest? Mrs. Deatherage is dying to know."

"I would say we are heading in the direction of an official engagement. We are working out a few details first."

Robert said, "I can't pin her down."

"Have you proposed properly?" Willie asked.

"And what is that, dear woman?"

"I don't know how they do it in merry old England, but one gets the father's permission before asking the intended bride."

"Mona's father is dead," Robert said.

Dexter interrupted Willie, "If the father agrees, then the gentleman will find a romantic occasion, get on one knee, and propose with a ring to signify the agreement. It's basically a contract."

Mona laughed. "Aren't you the romantic one?"

Robert scoffed, "A contract, indeed. What nonsense."

"I have had cases where those thrown over for another love have sued. I had one woman who sued her *intended* when he discovered someone more to his liking before the wedding. He broke it off with his fiancée and married another woman."

"The cad. Since the lawsuit became a public record, you can tell us who it was," Mona asked before taking a sip of coffee.

"You're looking at him," Dexter said.

Surprised, Mona spat her coffee out.

Robert clapped his hands together in glee before tugging the servant's cord. He was still laughing when Samuel entered the room. "Samuel, we need some club soda. Miss Mona has inadvertently spewed her coffee on Mr. Deatherage."

Samuel gave the group a strange look.

Dexter held up his hand. "Samuel, don't bother. I was going home anyway."

"You sure, Mr. Deatherage?" Samuel asked.

"Quite," Dexter replied, wiping his stained shirt and waistcoat with a napkin.

Samuel left the room, muttering to himself.

Willie hid behind her hands, giggling with abandonment.

"I'm so sorry, Dexter," Mona said, horribly embarrassed. She tried to help Dexter pat the coffee from his clothes.

He pushed her away. "Mona, you're making it worse."

Mona snapped, "Robert, would you quit laughing like a hyena?"

"I'm not the one who has to buy Dexter a new suit."

Mona wiped the coffee off the floor. "I feel like a fool, but it was such a surprise. Please forgive me, both of you."

Lowering her hands and now hiccuping from giggling, Willie said, "You're forgiven."

Robert poured Willie more coffee. "Take a sip and then count to ten. It will take away the hiccups."

Willie obliged him.

"You must tell me what happened," Mona said, now composed.

"I was engaged to a fine woman whom I thought I loved, and at the time did love. Three months before our wedding, I bumped into Willie downtown. Now we had known each other socially before that, but we had never spent any time alone together. She had been shopping and was going for some lunch. I don't know why, but I impulsively asked her if I could carry her packages and join her. She said yes. Before lunch was over, I had fallen hopelessly in love with my Wilhemina. I asked Willie out for several dates before I broke it off with my intended."

"You were a cad," Robert said, grinning.

"Yes, I was. I hurt a woman I loved and respected."

Glancing at Dexter's serious face, Robert quit joking. "I know the feeling, pal. I deeply hurt a lovely woman in my callous youth. Luckily, she forgave me and is happily married to someone else."

"What happened to your intended bride?" Mona asked.

Dexter said, "She sued for breach of contract."

"Did she win?" Mona asked.

Wille piped up, "Yes, she did and the scandal caused Dexter to be fired from his law firm."

"I was seen as flippant and unreliable. I was shut off socially as well. Mothers didn't want their daughters around me as I might corrupt them. This can be a very judgmental and unforgiving town."

"Why have you never told me?" Mona asked.

"It's a painful chapter in my history. Why dredge it up?"

"Why are you now?" Robert asked.

"Because my intended was Connie Hopper's sister—Consuelo."

7

"That's why you two weren't invited to Elspeth's reception. I wondered why you weren't there." Mona said.

"Guilty as charged," Willie said, placing her hand over Dexter's.

Robert said to Dexter, "And here I thought you were just an unimaginative sod when all the time you were hiding the soul of a Percy Shelley."

Dexter gave Robert a strange look. "Thank you, I guess?"

"Robert, save your breath to cool your soup," Mona said.

"Uh oh, I've said something wrong," Robert said. "Sorry, old man."

Dexter shook his head. "No offense taken, Robert. I know it's a strange story."

"That's why you were reluctant to take on Elspeth as a client," Mona said.

"Yes. Connie would see it as my interfering in his life again."

"What happened to Consuelo?" Robert asked.

"She's been married twice and resides in Venice. I don't think she's had a happy life."

"How unhappy can she be living in Venice?" Robert said.

Mona turned around in her seat. "I wish you were more respectful."

"That's my cue to leave. Chin chin," Robert said before leaning over and kissing Mona on the cheek.

After the door shut behind Robert, Willie said, "You do realize that Robert gets snide when he's uncomfortable with a subject."

"Yes, I know. Stiff upper lip and all that bull. I'm afraid your story about Consuelo brought back painful memories of Lady Alice. That's one of the reasons I'm holding off marrying Robert. He still needs to work through some issues."

Willie got up and sat next to Mona. "My dear, if you wait until everything is perfect and every issue settled, you might be waiting forever. Life is never perfect—nor are people."

"I love him so deeply it scares me, Willie. My love for Robert colors everything I say or do."

"Then marry Robert, Mona, and put the man out of his misery," Dexter said.

There was a knock on the door and Samuel entered. "Miss Mona, you asked to alert you for your three o'clock meeting."

Surprised, Mona looked at her wristwatch. "So late already."

Dexter stood. "I need to go home and change anyway. Come, my sweet, your Shelley must away."

"How do I love thee? Let me count the ways," Willie mused, letting Dexter pull her up.

Dexter said, "That's Elizabeth Barrett Browning, my dear, not Shelley."

Mona walked them to the front door. "This conversation is not over. I still have many questions about Elspeth and Consuelo."

"My lips are sealed," Dexter said.

"Dexter, you haven't even told me how my uncle came to hire you in the first place."

"Now, that's a story. I'll save it for another time."

"I'll hold you to it," Mona said, smiling and kissing Willie goodbye. She watched them drive away until the car rounded the bend and out-of-sight. She quietly shut the front door and locked it before heading to her office for a meeting with Mr. Thomas.

8

Mona and Thomas were going through the monthly household accounts. Mona had promoted Thomas from butler to household manager. It was now Thomas' job to procure all items for the house, budget the monthly expenditures, handle any repairs, and oversee all the house staff. In his spare time, Thomas trained Samuel to be a butler. Once a month, they went over the books together, and Mona signed the checks that Thomas prepared for her.

"Looks like our food budget is back in line this month," Mona said, scanning the tallies.

"Growing our own food has helped a lot. We still have carrots, potatoes, and beets stored in the ice house."

"How's the new hothouse doing?"

"We have plants growing, but the cost of heating it has increased dramatically. It would be better just to can the excess summer vegetables instead of using a hothouse in the winter."

"Let's give the hothouse a year and then reassess it. I want us to be as independent as possible. The local grocery stores are robbing us blind. We need to continue working on the food budget." Mona put down her pen. "How did the employees' garden work out?"

"We had a hard time keeping the deer out. They jump over any fence we put up. I wish you'd give us permission to hunt them."

"And end up accidentally shooting one of my Thoroughbreds? I should say not. This summer, let's move the garden closer to the equipment barn and plant two more acres of corn and a half-acre more of potatoes. We'll put another garden where there is one now and let the animals have at it."

"Won't solve the problem."

Mona sighed. She was exasperated with Thomas' negativity. He had been down for the last several months. "Thomas, you've seemed kind of somber the past few weeks. Is there something you are not telling me?"

"No, Miss Mona, but there is an opportunity I would like to discuss with you."

"What is it?"

"You know how you hold these teas on Thursdays and folks from the community ask you for help."

"Yes?"

"We have several bright young people in the black community who need financial assistance. They want to study to be doctors, but they don't have the resources to do so. I was wondering if you would help them a bit."

"Do you personally vouch for these young folks?"

"Yes, I do wholeheartedly. It wouldn't be much money. Just tuition and books."

"How are they going to eat?"

"They'll work."

"And go to school full-time! That's hard to do. I should know."

"You did it."

"Yes, I did work and go to school, but it's a struggle. I missed out on social activities and opportunities with my professors—extra credit, that type of thing because I couldn't forgo work."

"Miss Mona, will you help us?"

Mona flipped open her checkbook. "How much do you need?"

Thomas shook his head. "No checks, Miss Mona. Nothing that can be traced. Must be in cash."

"Cash? Isn't that a little irregular?"

"You can't tell anyone what the money is for. If the teller asks you why the withdrawal—lie. Put the money in a brown paper sack, and I'll get it to where it's supposed to go."

Mona studied Thomas' demeanor. She saw a man who had been born of a former slave from this very farm. His deeply-lined face showed all the battle scars of living in the South amongst white people who held all the power. Being a woman who worked in a "man's" profession, Mona had a few battle scars herself and until recently was banging her head against a wall trying to get a job. Now, as long as she had money, Mona had power and she was going to use that power to wipe a little injustice from her corner of the world. "Tell me how much you need."

"Six hundred dollars."

"I'll go to the bank in a few days and get it for you. Can you wait?"

"Yes."

"Is that everything?"

"Yes, Miss Mona. Thank you." Thomas collected his ledgers and left the office.

For a moment, Mona held her hand up to her heart. As with Elspeth, Mona felt Thomas was keeping something from her. She could just feel it. Something important had been left unsaid.

But what was it?

9

Mona was dining with Robert at his home when the housekeeper interrupted.

"Lord Farley, there is a man at the back door wishing to see you. He says it is of the utmost importance."

"Who is it?"

"He wouldn't give his name but he's a little black man."

Surprised, Robert and Mona glanced at each other.

"Please ask the gentleman to wait in the library and take him a plate. He must have missed his dinner. Also keep this visit to yourself. The rest of the staff doesn't need to know."

"Yes, Lord Farley," the housekeeper said, pursing her lips. She disapproved of having the dwarfish man in the house. The back stoop was a good enough place for someone the likes of him to wait, but she was hired to do her employer's bidding. She needed the job and wasn't going to do anything to jeopardize it. She had three kids to raise since her old man had run out.

"What do you think Jellybean wants?" Mona asked, once the housekeeper was out of earshot.

"Don't know. Let's finish dinner first. Otherwise, this pot roast will grow cold, and Cook will inquire as to why we didn't eat it."

Mona ate hurriedly, barely tasting the food. She knew Jellybean would not have shown up unless it was important. She and Robert threw down their napkins at the same time and rushed to the library where they found Jellybean eating at Robert's desk.

Looking up, Jellybean said, "Nice roast. Needs more salt, though."

Robert grinned. "I'll make sure to tell Cook."

"And you really need to lock the drawers on your desk. You have way too much money in your checking account. You never know when there might be a run on the banks again," Jellybean said, buttering a roll.

Mona stifled a laugh. After all, Jellybean was hired to be a snoop.

Robert pulled up two chairs for Mona and himself. "Why are you here, Jellybean? Something wrong?"

"I'll say. Look—I want to get out of town for a few days. I know how the sheriff from Woodford County is. He's as bad as Sheriff Monahan in this county. I need some money to get out of town."

"Why are you putting the touch on us?" Mona asked.

"Did you not recommend my services to the Hoppers? It is because of you two that I'm in trouble."

Robert thumbed at Mona. "It was her, not me."

Mona made a face at Robert. "Traitor."

"I need money to get out of town. Are you gonna help me or not?"

"Let's slow down for a moment," Robert said. "What happened?"

"Mrs. Hopper's maid, Beulah, was found dead this morning and, of course, the first people they suspect is us black folk. Since I was newly hired, they want to talk to me. Well, talking with this Sheriff means meetin' the wrong end of his big, ol' truncheon. No, thanks. I'll let you white folks sort this out."

Mona exclaimed, "Elspeth's maid is dead!"

"Wait a minute. Wait a minute," Robert said. "Let's focus. Are you saying the maid was murdered? How do you know she didn't die of natural causes?"

"Because she was found face down in a foot of snow with a kitchen knife stuck in her back," Jellybean announced. "That pretty much says murder in my book."

"That's dreadful. Tell us what happened," Mona said.

Robert poured Mona and Jellybean each a glass of bourbon. "Let's settle before the fire. This may take a while to sort out."

Jellybean sopped up the last of the roast gravy with a yeast roll before joining Mona and Robert in the comfy chairs before the fire. He savored a sip of the bourbon while closing his eyes. "Now, that's some nice hooch. Goes down smooth. Not like the usual rotgut I have to swill."

Mona said, "Start at the beginning. You got

word that Mrs. Hopper wanted you to do some work for her."

"That's right. Her cook sent word to me, and I came after breakfast two weeks ago. We met in the mud room where Mrs. Hopper proceeds to tell me about the threatening letters. She was concerned her stepson had sent them."

"She never confided that to me," Mona said. "This is new."

"Why suspect Cadwallader Hopper?" Robert asked.

"I can't get into that. Mrs. Hopper's my client. Of course, she's never paid me a dime, so if you paid me what I'm owed, then you would be my client, and I could tell ya. I mean it was your idea that she contact me."

Robert pulled out his wallet and said, "You are the devil, Jellybean. How much?"

"Three hundred will do."

"Three hundred dollars!" Mona exclaimed.

"Lord Farley, you should have the extra money in the locked box you keep in the second drawer on the left of your desk. I also want the promise of a criminal lawyer if I should need one. If I had known that trouble like murder was in the Hopper house I never would have taken the gig. You should have warned me that this case was going to be like a breeze comin' off an outhouse."

"How were we supposed to know Beulah would get knocked off?" Mona argued.

"You can smell murder in the air," Jellybean said.

"Then you should have smelled it yourself," Mona retorted.

Robert got up and took a key out of his vest pocket and unlocked his petty cash box. Counting out bills, he handed them to Jellybean who put the money in his sock before taking another sip of bourbon.

Satisfied, Jellybean continued his tale of woe. "The household staff is a wreck. No one has a permanent job description except for the cook. We all pitch in where we can. I was hired as kitchen staff, but I was cleaning out the fireplaces, serving the meals, repairing things here and there, helping the maid change the beds, even dusting. It was crazy, man. I should never have been on the second floor, but I was. The po-po will find my fingerprints on the second floor."

"If Beulah was found outside, why would finding your fingerprints on the second floor of the house be of such concern? I would think that fingerprints on the knife would be of the utmost importance," Robert said.

Mona placed her hand on Robert's. "Frankly, dear. You know how things work here in the South."

"Why don't they have a housekeeper?" Robert asked, turning her attention back to Jellybean.

"Can't keep one. Mrs. Hopper will give instructions and then Mr. Hopper will come right after and contradict her. He wants things done his way. It sure has caused some serious fights because there are too many cats in the litter box. Nothing can get done. Those two keep changing the housekeeper's instructions, so the ladies quit because of the chaos. They've gone through three housekeepers I'm told and two maids since Mrs. Hopper arrived."

"Who is running the house, then?" Mona asked.

"The cook is at the moment, and she's getting fed up with the situation. Her job is to put food on the table—not to run the household."

Robert said, "There is a lot of stress in the house?"

Jellybean bobbed his head. "Puttin' it mildly."

"What is Mrs. Hopper's demeanor?" Mona asked.

"Quiet. Trying to establish herself, but going about it the wrong way."

"What do you mean?" Mona asked.

"She was always walking the long way around the barn."

"Is this the American way of saying that instead of telling Mr. Hopper what she wants, Mrs. Hopper is making him guess?" Robert said.

"Exactly. I realize it came across as though he was trying to undermine her by going behind her back, but Mr. Hopper was trying to help."

Robert looked pleased that he was finally understanding the Kentucky natives.

"I'm not sure what you're driving at, Jellybean," Mona said.

"Being from another country and culture, Mrs. Hopper doesn't understand how we do things here in Kentucky. She is overly fussy and rude. She takes her frustrations out on the staff."

"Give me an example."

Jellybean said, "This leaps to mind. She caught one of the upstairs maids sampling one of her perfumes. Mrs. Hopper told the maid to slap herself in the face for stealing. The maid refused and quit. I don't blame her. Imagine telling someone to hit themselves for dabbing on a bit of fragrance. Everyone knows that the maids will use a bit of their mistress' perfume and makeup. It's expected."

Robert and Mona stared at each other. He asked of Mona, "Is this a cultural thing?"

"People from all cultures can be harsh with their employees, but I did see this type of rebuke far more prevalent in the Near East," Mona said.

Robert turned to Jellybean. "What you are saying is that Mrs. Hopper doesn't get along with the staff. Doesn't that make her a prime suspect in Beulah's murder?"

"Mrs. Hopper relied on her, and Beulah seemed to adore Mrs. Hopper. I think Beulah was Mrs. Hopper's one true friend. I doubt Mrs. Hopper had anything to do with Beulah's murder. Stabbing someone doesn't seem to be a woman's way of committing murder. Women like to use guns or poison."

Mona asked, "What do you think happened?"

"Things started to heat up when the prodigal son, Cadwallader Hopper, turned up."

Robert said, stoking the fire, "So Wally Hopper is back."

Jellybean made a face. "He's a mean one for sure—like potato salad left out on a hot day. He's a spoiler."

"When did he arrive?" Mona asked.

"Five days ago and the tension got thicker."

Mona said, "Tell us about him."

"You know how the Bible tells us that pride goeth before a fall? Well, this man should have tripped into some manure long before now."

"He is a nasty, little prat—a real wanker," Robert added.

Both Mona and Jellybean raised their eyebrows in surprise. Lord Farley was using a word not spoken in polite society.

"Tell us how you really feel, Robert," Mona said, smirking.

"Sorry, my dear, but that boy gets my dander up."

"I've heard worse."

"I will never sell a horse to Wally Hopper. He

races his horses on the circuit until they drop from exhaustion and then he sells them to a glue factory. He has no respect for the animals or the racing industry."

Mona didn't reply. Until the racing industry adopted more humane policies, she wasn't going to race. All her stallions had been put out to pasture, and Mooncrest Farm only boarded mares and foals. Most owners treated their horses with respect, but Mona had seen enough of the "others" to know that racing had a dark underbelly. She wanted no part of it, having seen enough cruelty to last her a lifetime, but she and Robert didn't agree on the subject. Racing, as well as pleasure riding, was a passion of his, but then Robert provided wonderful care for his horses.

Robert said, "Let's start with Cadwallader coming home."

"He just showed up and immediately started haranguing Mrs. Hopper. She would break out into tears and hide in her room."

"In what way did Wally criticize her?" Mona asked.

"I don't know how to explain it, but it would seem he was complimenting Mrs. Hopper but it was backwards."

"Like a backhanded compliment?" Mona asked.

"I guess you could call it that." Jellybean thumbed his lip. "When I was serving one time, he told Mrs. Hopper she looked exceptionally pretty that night—that is for a wog."

Mona gasped. "That's unseemly. What happened?"

"Mrs. Hopper threw her napkin on the table and left the dining hall in a snit and Mr. Hopper proceeded to upbraid his son."

"Righto," Robert said. "I hope Connie set his son straight."

"Cadwallader laughed his head off. Frustrated that he wasn't getting through to his son, Mr. Hopper went in search of his wife. Nobody can teach that boy any manners. He does what he wants because he holds all the cards."

"That is until his father married Mrs. Hopper. Connie's pretty flush now, isn't he?" Robert asked.

"Hopper Sr. wants Mrs. Hopper to sell her father's collection of Egyptian antiquities and she won't budge. The income from her trust fund keeps them in chocolate and stockings, but not for big extravagances."

"I understood her money would last way past her children's lives," Mona said.

Jellybean arched his eyebrows. "Not if she goes spending it on fancy cars and a racing stable. That would run her dry in years. Besides, Mrs. Hopper is scared to death that if she lets loose of the purse strings, Hopper Sr. will start gambling again."

Robert said, "I thought that was his father's sin."

Jellybean held out his empty glass and waggled it. "It seems hubby has a little gambling problem, too. Found out Mrs. Hopper paid off his gambling debts in London before they got married."

"How did Cadwallader treat his mother?" Mona asked, changing the subject.

"Haven't a clue. She died while the boy was young."

"Is Cadwallader married?" Mona asked.

Jellybean shook his head. "Not that I'm aware of. He doesn't seem to like women, at least the females in his house, both upstairs and downstairs."

Robert asked, "How does he treat the female staff?"

"Very curt, but he leaves them alone as long as they do as ordered. He doesn't badger them sexually if that's what you mean."

Mona leaned forward in her chair. "What about Beulah?"

"Beulah practically hissed when she saw him. Cadwallader would do things like bump into her on purpose if they passed in the hallway—then apologize profusely as if it was an accident. It got so bad, Beulah would flatten herself against the wall as he walked by."

Mona asked, "Didn't Beulah use the servant's staircase?"

"No. Beulah acted as though she was mistress of the house. She used the front door for her comin's and goin's—never the servant's door. Never ate with the rest of the servants. Ate in her room while Mrs. Hopper had meals downstairs."

"That's a chore to carry a heavy tray up and down a staircase six times a day. I don't recall the Hoppers having an elevator," Mona said.

"They don't."

"Maybe she stayed upstairs to keep away from

Wally." Robert asked, "Who prepared her food?"

"Beulah did, but she ate light. Mostly fruit and vegetables with rice."

"Who prepared the family's food?" Mona asked.

"The cook."

"Was there ever an explanation for why Beulah didn't take her meals with the rest of the house employees?"

Jellybean shook his head. "No."

"How did the rest of the staff get along with her?"

"We were mostly standoffish. To be honest, we didn't have much contact with Beulah. She was Mrs. Hopper's employee—not one of the house employees. Mrs. Hopper paid Beulah out of her own pocket and not from the household accounts."

Mona looked stymied for a moment. "I don't know what for. Beulah was not a good maid. Mrs. Hopper came to tea at Moon Manor with a run in her stocking and hair on her clothes. What maid would allow that? It's a blight on her reputation. Also on the night of the reception, I was in Mrs. Hopper's boudoir, and I never saw hide nor hair of this Beulah. Did Beulah accompany Mrs. Hopper outside the house as a companion?"

"Yes. Everywhere Mrs. Hopper went, Beulah was always her shadow."

"Again, this surprises me because Mrs. Hopper came to Moon Mansion for tea, and I never saw Beulah nor did my staff report that she stopped in the kitchen for refreshments. Tell me, Jellybean, what did she look like?"

"Except for her coloring, she looked like a carbon copy of Mrs. Hopper."

"Elaborate," Mona demanded.

"Mrs. Hopper has dark coloring and is petite. Beulah was taller, lighter-skinned, and dark blonde, but the features were strikingly similar."

"I see," Mona exhaled. "Tell me something, Jellybean. Did you think Mrs. Hopper was being physically abused?"

"I never saw anything like that. Sometimes I would hear Mr. Hopper raise his voice with her, and they'd go at it, but never saw him being rough with her. If he was, one of the maids would have mentioned seeing something."

"What about Wally?" Robert asked.

"He was just plain mean with his mouth.

Never saw him go near Mrs. Hopper."

"But he was aggressive with Beulah it seems," Mona said.

Jellybean stood. "I best be going. There's a train leaving at eleven. I intend to be on it."

Mona reached for the telephone. "Don't. If the Sheriff is looking for you, he'll certainly have men at the train depot. Let my man, Jamison drive you to the Union Terminal in Cincinnati. They won't be looking there."

"No thanks. I have a cousin who works for the railroad. He'll sneak me on. No one will ever know. I'll be in touch when the murderer is caught." Jellybean picked up his peacock feathered hat and coat. "I'll show myself out. Thanks for the supper. I saw fruit on the dining table. I'll be taking a few apples on the way out."

"Chin chin," Robert said, looking perplexed.

After a few moments, Mona picked up the dinner tray and took it into the kitchen, which had already been cleaned and put up from dinner. Mona washed the dishes and put them up in the cupboard.

Robert leaned against the icebox. "A woman's work is never done. My bedroom needs a good dusting, too."

Mona, deep in thought, turned to Robert. "Don't you think Jellybean's description of Beulah is interesting?"

"In what way?"

"Except for the coloring, they looked similar."

"So what?"

"So, I think that is interesting."

Robert reached over and pulled Mona to him. "I'll tell you what's interesting. The servants are all gone now. We are totally alone. No one to spy on us."

Mona looked at her watch. "Oh, gosh. I've got to go. Violet is waiting up for me."

Robert wouldn't let Mona loose from his grip. "You're not putting me off, missy. It's always rush, rush, rush with you."

Mona smiled. "It's always kiss, kiss, kiss with you."

"Someone has to remember the important things we need to do." Robert cupped her chin. "Let's announce our engagement. Let's set a date. Whaddya say?"

"Now who's rushing?"

Robert feigned hurt. "You're a big tease."

Mona laughed and kissed Robert on the

cheek. "You're a big baby. I'll give you lots of kisses tomorrow, but I must beg off now."

Robert brightened at the promise of more kisses. "Let me get my coat."

"No need to walk me home. The moon is still bright."

"Call me when you get in so I know you're safe."

"I will, darling."

"Love me?"

"Robert, I simply adore you." Mona placed her hand on her heart. "Swear it."

"Then you may go, Madame." Robert released her and helped her with her coat. "Remember, call me when you get in."

"I promise." Mona gave Robert one last kiss on his lips, but as soon as she was out the door, she thought about what Jellybean had said. Elspeth and Beulah had looked similar.

10

The next sunny afternoon, Mona, Violet, and Dotty squeezed in the back seat of the Daimler merrily chatting.

"I'm only going to be about a half-hour, ladies," Mona said. "Just a quick trip to the bank and then home."

"That will give me enough time to run to the five-and-dime. I need some black thread. Miss Mona is awfully hard on her clothes."

Mona piped in, "That's true. Violet keeps me looking respectable."

"They got some new material as well," Violet chirped.

"What are you going to make?" asked Dotty, who was Mona's personal secretary.

"A new spring frock."

"Spring seems so far away!" Dotty said. "Winter can be so dreary."

"I want to be ready. It was in the paper that the five-and-dime has new cottons in. I want a nice dress with white cuffs on three-quarter sleeves and white piping for the trim." Violet pulled a dress pattern out of her purse. "It will look like this."

"Very pretty," Mona said, looking at the drawing on the pattern envelope.

Violet explained to Dotty. "It's to be my high school graduation dress. I had to quit school to work when the hard times hit, but Miss Mona hired a tutor for me and I've been keeping up with my school work. I'm going to take the equivalency exam and hopefully pass. If I do, I will have my high school diploma." Violet's eyes brightened at the thought.

"You will with flying colors," Dotty said, reassuringly.

"My mother is going to make a cake and have a small celebration. You all are welcome to come."

"Wouldn't miss it for the world," Mona said, clasping Violet's hands.

"I'll think I'll join you at the five-and-dime, Violet. I need some lace for a slip," Dotty said.

"Since we are back on clothes, did either of you see Elspeth Hopper when she came to tea?" Mona asked.

Violet hesitated a second before she spoke. "I saw her from the top of the stairs when she was leaving."

"What was your impression, Violet?" Mona asked.

"Her suit was very smart, but the wrong green for her skin color. Made her look waxy."

"Anything else?"

"She had a run in her stocking and the houndstooth coat was all wrong for her handbag."

"What do you mean, Violet? A purse is a purse," Dotty said.

"Maybe for you and me, but not for a lady who spends a great deal of money on her attire. Mrs. Hopper should put more effort into her accessories."

Mona shrugged when Dotty shot her a quick look. "I just dress in whatever Violet picks out for me."

Dotty snorted. "I know that's not true."

"Women should always pick purses and gloves to match their coat—not their dress, and Mrs. Hopper's gloves and purse were not of the same color."

"You mean one's gloves should match the purse also?" Dotty asked. "If that's true, then I'm in a world of trouble. I buy what I can afford."

"That's true of most women in these troubled times. However, Mrs. Hopper lived in London, traveled through New York and Cincinnati, where she would have shopped."

"Maybe she doesn't care about fashion," Mona offered.

"A woman, newly married to a fussbucket like Mr. Hopper, not want to impress her husband?" Violet shook her head. "I don't know a single woman who wouldn't try to dress to make her new husband proud."

Mona took in Violet's impressions. "I've gotta ask. What do you think of a maid who would let her mistress leave the house in such a state as Mrs. Hopper?"

"She's not a proper maid. Look here." Violet pulled out two rolled balls of muslin and opened one. "I always keep extra stockings in my purse—one for Miss Mona and one for me—just in case we should get a run in our hose while we are out."

Dotty leaned over and peered into Violet's purse. "What else you got in the satchel of yours?"

Violet snapped her purse shut. "Make fun if you want, but I keep the tools of my trade in here."

"I'm curious, too," Mona said. "What do you consider tools of your trade?"

"I have a sewing kit, several handkerchiefs, two tubes of lipstick of different reds for Miss Mona, peppermint candies for bad breath and upset stomach, and two compacts of different shades."

"Why two compacts?" Mona asked.

"We wear different shades, so one is for me and the other for you because you are always forgetting your face powder. I also keep small bills and coins in money because you always have big bills for which some businesses can't provide change."

Mona looked stunned at Dotty, "Good grief, I had no idea. It makes me sound like I need a nanny when I leave the house."

Violet leaned back in the seat looking smug.

"From what I saw, I would say that her maid was not a trained lady's maid at all."

"You may be right. I remember Mrs. Hopper saying she had hired the woman to help when her mother became ill. Maybe she is really a nurse and a companion. Perhaps, we assumed incorrectly that she was Mrs. Hopper's maid when she wasn't at all."

Dotty asked, "Then who is Mrs. Hopper's maid? A woman in her position always has someone to look after her clothes and things."

"I can find out," Violet said.

"Look at you," Mona teased. "Where's that shy girl I met when I first came here? Where is my Violet and what have you done with her?"

Violet giggled.

"How do you propose to do so?" Dotty asked.

"All I have to do is look at the maid's room. I'll be able to tell," Violet said with firm conviction.

"I'll see if I can make that happen," Mona said.

Violet spied her store in the distance and tapped on the window to Jamison, Mona's chauffeur. "Jamison, let us off at the next corner, please." She turned to Mona. "Miss Mona, why don't you meet us at the five-and-dime? They make wonderful milkshakes."

"Ooh, I could go for a chocolate sundae with nuts and a cherry on top," Dotty said.

Mona said, "Sounds like a plan. I'll meet you both in half-a-hour."

Violet and Dotty scurried out of the car.

Mona watched Violet excitedly enter the store. It wouldn't be long before the timid girl with gangly limbs and an awkward demeanor would metamorphose into a confident young woman with her whole life before her. In fact, Violet was transforming into a butterfly right before Mona's eyes. Any vestige of that young girl would disappear soon.

Suddenly, Mona felt sad and bewildered. She was going to miss the naive girl who loved to sew and prattle about the latest Harlow and Gable movie. Mona realized she hated to see Violet grow up.

Right now, Violet had lipstick, candy, and a sewing kit in her purse.

Mona carried a gun in her purse.

That was the difference between being a youngster and a woman in Mona's world.

11

Mona walked into the bank and asked for the manager. Waiting for him, she noticed the black and white marble floor and walls with the tall ceilings held up by massive, marble fluted columns. The odors of disinfectant, cologne, ink, and money wafted through the lobby. While no one spoke above a whisper, there was a murmuring of human voices and the unmistakable sound of rubber stamps documenting bank books of their withdrawals or deposits.

A lanky man with a thin, pencil mustache came out and invited Mona into his office. He held the door open and beckoned her to a chair before shutting the door. "What can I do for you, Miss Moon?" he asked, looking her over.

Mona ignored his leer. She was used to men

staring at her, but she didn't like it and it immediately put her back up. "I called ahead and requested six-hundred dollars in small bills."

"That's quite a bit of money."

"Yes."

Seeing that Mona was not going to add to her simple declaration, the bank manager pulled on his vest and smiled a greasy grin. "We need to make sure that you are not being coerced into withdrawing this money."

"I understand your concern."

"I'll just make a call to Dexter Deatherage. After all, that is quite a bit of money for a little lady to carry around. We usually don't let wives withdraw such large amounts from the bank."

"Excuse me? I'm not married and this is my money from my personal account."

"Still, you must understand the bank's policy."

Mona fumed, "No, I don't. If a woman's name is on the account, she should be able to withdraw any amount she wishes without her husband's permission—or any man's permission."

The bank manager gave Mona a condescending smile. "I would love to explain our bank's economic policy to you—maybe over a cup of coffee—or even dinner."

"You do understand that I run Mooncrest Enterprises plus Mooncrest Farm. I have thousands of employees who work for me."

The bank manager pulled up a little bit. "Well, I'm sure Dexter helps you make the right decisions."

"Dexter Deatherage works for me. I tell *him* what to do—not the other way around. As for your fear of my being coerced, let me reassure you." Mona pulled a pistol from her purse and pointed it at the bank manager. "Do you find this convincing?"

Startled, the bank manager threw up his hands. He had heard stories about Mona Moon being a wild card, but this was unseemly. "Please, Miss Moon! We have your money ready." Nervously, he pulled an envelope from his desk and handed it over.

Mona put the gun as well as the envelope in her purse. "Thank you for your cooperation." She stood and left the office, but before she could leave the bank, a man approached her.

"Miss Moon, may I speak with you?" he

asked, taking off his hat. He held a Stetson hat with both hands, but Mona could tell he was packing a shoulder holster. There was a bulge under his left armpit.

"My bodyguards are right outside the door."

"I know. I saw them and your car. That black and red Daimler is unmistakable. That's why I followed you in here."

Mona looked nervously around the bank lobby. Could she reach her gun before he pulled his?"

"I have identification. Please allow me to go into my left breast pocket." The man slowly reached in his coat pocket and pulled out a badge.

Mona leaned over and studied it.

"My name is Sheriff Joshua Gideon. I am investigating the murder of Beulah Bradley. I would like to talk with you, if I might?"

Mona rocked back on her heels. "The Hoppers live in another county. You're in Fayette County."

"That's right. They live in Woodford County. That makes it my jurisdiction." The Sheriff looked around and noticed a small cluster of chairs near the front window. "Let's sit over there, shall we?" He cupped Mona's elbow and led her over.

Smiling, he said, "This should give us some privacy. That bank manager over there looks a little green around the gills. Let's turn our chairs toward the window. He doesn't need to hear us talking."

Mona glanced over at the bank manager who was watching them. "The little weasel. He tried to insert himself into my business."

"I take it you don't like that."

"No, Sheriff Gideon. I don't like men blowing smoke up my skirt."

"I heard that you were a woman of—hmm, how shall I say this—an independent streak."

"How can I help you, Sheriff? I know nothing about Beulah Bradley's death."

"I understand you were a guest at Mrs. Hopper's reception."

"So were several hundred other people."

"But they did not go upstairs."

"I asked one of the maids if I could use the upstairs powder room."

"So you don't deny it?"

"Why would I deny it?"

"Why not use the bathrooms downstairs?"

"Because they were in use."

"I see."

"I don't. Where are you going with this? What does my having to use the upstairs powder room have to do with Beulah's death? That reception was weeks ago."

"Tell me what happened when you went upstairs."

"I went upstairs, used the bathroom, fixed my makeup, and came down."

"Did you see anyone upstairs?"

"Yes, I ran into Mrs. Hopper."

"And?"

"And what?"

"Miss Moon, please don't fence with me. What happened when you saw Mrs. Hopper?"

"She wanted to change her dress, so I selected a red gown for her and helped her dress. End of story."

"What was Mrs. Hopper's demeanor?"

"Ask Mrs. Hopper."

"I'm asking you, Miss Moon."

"I have a hard time discerning other people's emotions, Sheriff Gideon."

"I see. Did you see Beulah Bradley?"

"I saw no one else."

"And you saw no one else upstairs?"

"I just said that."

"Isn't it usual for a lady's maid to wait in her mistress' room to assist with a dress change during a party in case of a mishap?"

"I don't know what Mrs. Hopper's staff requirements are. My maid will lend a hand with a party, but she is ready to assist me if I need help."

Sheriff Gideon flipped his hat in his hands, thinking.

Mona remained quiet, studying the man and the hat which was brown, showing signs of wear but was recently brushed. As for the man—the sheriff was young—in his mid-thirties with dark hair and hazel eyes. Mona caught the scent of Aqua Velva cologne on his freshly-shaven face. She also observed that the Sheriff's collar was a little frayed but the shirt was starched and pressed. His hands were calloused, but the fingers were long and slender and with the fingernails clean and trimmed. He wore a shiny, gold wedding band on his left hand and it looked loose, making Mona wonder if the Sheriff had lost weight recently. All in all, Sheriff Gideon seemed to be a man who cared about his appearance, and Mona imagined that when he had money he bought the best.

"I understand Mrs. Hopper came to your house."

"I invited her to tea the next day."

"Did she come?"

"Yes."

"What did you two talk about?"

"Sheriff, am I suspected of a crime?"

"No, Miss Moon. Just gathering information. Is there some reason you don't want to tell me what you two talked about?"

"I don't like people prying into my personal business, and I doubt Mrs. Hopper would appreciate my sharing the contents of a private conversation. You need to ask her."

"People who put up a fuss usually have something to hide."

Mona stifled a laugh. She had been caught. Still, she was not going to show her hand so easily. She had learned that talking to the law was like playing poker. One always keeps one's cards close to the chest. "We talked about her marriage."

"What about it?"

"She was concerned about her happiness with Mr. Hopper. She felt she was failing him in some manner."

"In what way?"

"She felt Mr. Hopper disapproved of her."

"Why would he think that?"

"I wouldn't know. I am not privy to Cornelius Hopper's state of mind"

"Hmm. Anything else you two discussed?"

"She talked about staging an exhibition of her father's collection in Cincinnati."

"Did Mrs. Hopper discuss Miss Bradley?"

"The woman's name never came up."

"Did you see Miss Bradley that day?"

"No."

"When did you last communicate with Mrs. Hopper?"

"At my tea."

"No phone calls? No visits? Letters?"

"I haven't seen nor talked with Mrs. Hopper since she was at my house for tea."

"What about Miss Bradley?"

"I've never laid eyes on the unfortunate woman. Wouldn't know her if she walked right past me. Of course, that won't happen now."

Sheriff Gideon handed Mona a business card. "That's my office number. Call if you think of anything."

"Just a minute, Sheriff. Quid pro quo. I've given you information. Now I'd like a little myself. What did Beulah's autopsy find?"

"I can't discuss that with the public, Miss Moon."

"Was her death a homicide?"

"That I can tell you—yes. I'm looking for a killer."

"I heard Beulah was found outside in the snow with a knife stuck in her back."

Sheriff Gideon narrowed his eyes. "How would you know that? The manner of her death was not reported in the papers."

"I have connections, too, Sheriff. When exactly was Beulah Bradley murdered?"

"Two nights ago. Where were you? Quid pro quo, Miss Moon. Quid pro quo."

"At a dinner party with Lord Farley as my escort. I have plenty of witnesses."

"Where were you after the dinner party?"

Mona raised an eyebrow. "So she was killed in the wee hours of the next day."

Sheriff Gideon sighed and his right index finger twitched. He was tired of crossing swords with this woman. She was slick answering his questions—too slick. He wanted to get home. "Where were you, Miss Moon?"

"I was with Lord Farley."

"All night?"

"I would say a good portion of it."

Sheriff Gideon blushed. He couldn't believe a decent woman would admit to such behavior. "Is that the truth?"

"Shall I swear on the Bible?"

"Your word is good enough." Sheriff Gideon abruptly stood and donned his hat. "One last thing. Do you know a Jellybean Martin?"

"Who?"

"A small black man who is hired by you rich folks to cover up your dirty laundry. He's known for wearing a black fedora with a peacock feather."

"I have a laundress who sees to my laundry, Sheriff Gideon, and if that is not enough, I have a top-notch lawyer to see to my other needs."

Sheriff Gideon tipped his hat. "My wife is ill, so I need to get home. Until we meet again, Miss Moon, good day to you."

"Good-bye, Sheriff. I hope you catch your man."

Mona gave the Sheriff a moment to exit the bank before she, too, left the building meeting her bodyguards outside the bank. They followed Mona in a car behind the Daimler and waited for her outside the bank.

"Everything okay, Boss?" one of the Pinkerton agents asked.

"Yes," Mona replied, watching Sheriff Gideon walk down the street. "Boys, I'm going to the five-and-dime to meet the ladies for some ice cream. I would appreciate it if you would not stick out like a sore thumb. Try to blend in."

"We'll do our best, Miss Moon," one of agents replied.

Mona crossed the street and walked down half of a block to the five-and-dime. She had already pushed the interview from her mind and was thinking about a strawberry milkshake when she noticed Sheriff Gideon watching her from the next street corner. Mona hurried past the store's doors and made her way to Dexter's office. Looking at her wristwatch, she figured she could still catch him at the office on the next street over.

12

"You said what?" Dexter placed his head in his hands and moaned. "It's one thing to keep your Aunt Melanie out of trouble, but I expect so much more from you. Your behavior is becoming more and more reckless, Mona. What's gotten into you?"

"I know, Dexter, but I didn't want Sheriff Gideon to know about my connection to Jelly-bean Martin. I've had enough of my name in the paper the last month because of what happened in Eastern Kentucky."

"I kept most of it out."

"Yes, you did and I thank you for it."

Dexter tapped his desk with his index finger. "Don't you see? He already knew the answers before he asked the questions. He wouldn't have asked you about Jellybean Martin out of the clear blue sky. He purposely bushwhacked you at the bank to shake you up a bit."

"How would he know about Jellybean?"

"Mrs. Hopper has probably already told him that you made the recommendation. It was stupid to lie. Sheriff Gideon can charge you with obstruction."

"I didn't lie. I just learned a long time ago never to admit anything to the police."

"I never knew you were so anti-police, and the truth be told, Mona, you are splitting hairs."

"I'm not."

"It doesn't work that way down here, Mona. You've got to learn to get along with the lawmen in this area."

"After my experience with Sheriff Monahan regarding the death of Judge Garrett, I don't want to get to know them."

"Well, regardless of how you feel, you need to incorporate them into your life. Otherwise, they'll take their resentment out on your employees—and let me tell you, they can make it rough."

"Are you referring to the Klan? Are you saying the law down here backs the Klan?"

"I don't know and I don't want to know about that. I'm just telling you how things are."

"What do you think about Sheriff Joshua Gideon's name?"

"What about it?"

"He has the names of two biblical warriors. Joshua led the Israelites back into the Promise Land and tore down the walls of Jericho with the sound of rams' horns, and Gideon was a judge who fought the Midianites."

"So?"

Mona tossed her head. "I was wondering if Sheriff Gideon is like his namesakes. If so, then he will be formidable. He won't stop until he finds Beulah Bradley's murderer."

"Stay out of the man's way."

"I intend to." Mona picked up her purse. "I should go now."

"There's the other matter."

"Yes?"

"Did you pull a gun on the bank manager today? I got a call from the bank a half-hour ago."

"I most certainly did not. I pulled out my gun to show the bank manager that I could take care of myself and was not being unfairly coerced into withdrawing money."

"He says you pulled the gun on him."

"He's a liar. I don't like smug men who think they can intimidate me. He was trying to put the make on me. I've known men like him all my life. They smile to your face and then try to hammer you down by asserting themselves over you. They claim they are superior by nature or they use religion or they use their fists if the other two rationales don't work. I could tell the moment I met him that he was such a man."

"Okay. I'll smooth it out. I know he's a worm. He goes to my church."

"I don't want his version of events getting around."

"I'll kindly suggest to him that you take your privacy very seriously and would take offense if he was to spread his account of this afternoon's meeting—even to the point of litigation and switching banks. If he wants to keep his job, he'll keep his mouth shut."

"Let's just buy the bank."

"What?"

"If we have the money, let's buy the bank.

The manager made the assertion that female customers can't make large withdrawals without their husbands' permission. I bet men don't have to get their wives' permission to get money out of their joint account. I want to change the policy of the bank."

"Banks are a bad investment right now. Let me make the suggestion to the president of the bank that you would like that policy changed. He'll listen since you are the largest depositor."

"Thank you." Mona rose.

"I'm not finished."

"Dotty and Violet are waiting for me."

"They can wait. There's one other matter with the Sheriff."

"What's that?"

"You're not to talk with him again without me present."

"I understand."

"I don't know what's gotten into you, but you better settle down. You're stirring the pot too much."

"So says a man."

"So says this man who wants to protect you so he can keep his job. This community is very conservative. They don't like outside meddlers, and they consider you a Yankee trying to shove your extreme liberal agenda down their throats."

"I hardly think advocating women's rights as liberal. It is justice. I'm just pushing that along a little bit. Why should women always get the short end of the money stick? We have the right to vote now. The world is changing, and this community has got to change with it. Policies, which keep women economically repressed, should be abolished. We will never be true equal partners if we can't be financially independent from men."

"I don't disagree, but do we have to change the world today?"

Mona laughed. "I'll try to restrain myself the rest of this week."

"Mona, I'm on your side. I know we have problems, but people in Lexington are deeply religious. Many believe that a woman's place is in the home and the man should make all the decisions—and those same people sit on bank boards."

"Believe me, Dexter, when I threaten to change banks if that policy is not overturned, the bank board will have a sudden change of heart."

"I'll give it go," Dexter said, pointing a finger at Mona, "but you stay out of it and give me time. I need to do this in my own way. I'll make it their idea, dropping little hints here and there."

Mona grinned. "All right, Dexter. I'll try to stay out of mischief, but I'm not taking bull from anyone."

Dexter walked Mona out to the hallway where the Pinkerton men were waiting. "At least, you are following my suggestion about having bodyguards with you."

"Of course. They're helpful for carrying my packages when needed."

Dexter shot a look of despair at the Pinkerton men before going back into his office.

Mona marched out of the Mooncrest Building toward the five-and-dime all the time seething. All her life, men had tried to fence her in—tell her what to do, what to think, and even how she should look. She understood Elspeth Hopper's need to get out from under her husband's thumb. It was a desperation she recognized as she had felt it herself many times.

No matter what, Mona was never going to let a man rule over her!

13

Jamison helped Dotty, Violet, and finally Mona out of the car. Samuel held the front door open as the first two ladies ran up the steps with their packages chatting away.

Mona lingered, then walked back to the plain black Ford behind the Daimler. "Thank you, gentlemen, for keeping us safe," she said to the two Pinkerton men. Mona knew that letting employees know they were appreciated was important. She just didn't like being followed everywhere and secretly hoped this policy would run its course someday, but she had to admit that Dexter was right. It was a dangerous world at the moment, and she needed to take care. The men tipped their hats and drove off to the garage.

As Mona climbed the stairs past the stone

lions, she saw Samuel give her a warning signal with his two fingers tapping on his thigh. "What is it, Samuel?"

"Mrs. Hopper is in the drawing room waiting for you."

Mona looked around. "Where's her car?"

"In the garage being washed. It was awfully dirty."

"How long has she been waiting?"

"Almost an hour."

"Thank you, Samuel. I'll see her now. Have her car brought around," Mona said, handing Samuel her coat and purse. "Put my purse on the desk in my study and have Thomas interrupt me in ten minutes. I don't care what the excuse is."

"I will tell Mr. Thomas."

"Thank you, Samuel." Mona looked in the hallway mirror and patted down her platinum hair. Straightening her skirt and checking the seams on her stockings, Mona gave her appearance a nod and hurried into the drawing room. There she found a seated Elspeth wringing a handkerchief. Elspeth's eyes were red from weeping. Black mascara streaked down her cheeks, and her widow's bun had become undone with wisps of dark hair falling to her shoulders. Chloe, Mona's poodle, sat beside Elspeth and nuzzled the woman's hands in a gesture of comfort.

"Elspeth, please forgive me. I was going to come to you, but thought you needed some time first." Mona patted her thigh before taking a seat. "Chloe, come here."

"Oh, please don't. She's been keeping me company." Elspeth ran her hand along Chloe's back. "Her fur is so soft."

"Chloe is a comfort. She was my Uncle Manfred's dog, and now she has claimed me as well."

"I notice there are many dogs around your estate."

"Many of the workers bring their dogs with them. Believe me—Chloe is never lonely, and of course, we have the usual barn cats, chickens, and whatnots. You name it, it seems we're feeding it."

"That's nice. Your house feels like a home. Has a nice feeling to it."

"Thank you."

Elspeth paused for a moment and then asked, "Has Sheriff Gideon been to see you?"

"I just talked with him this afternoon."

"Did he bring up Jellybean Martin?"

"I'm afraid he did."

"What did you tell him?"

"Not much."

"He's pressing me about him, but I didn't know what to say."

"Tell Sheriff Gideon the truth the next time he asks."

Elspeth's eyes widened. "Really? Even about the letters?"

"Especially about the letters. I'm sure it has occurred to you that Beulah's death might be connected to those letters."

"No, it hasn't."

Mona sighed. Could Elspeth really be that dimwitted or was she pretending to be naive? "Did Beulah read the letters?"

"No."

"Where do you keep the letters?"

"Locked in my vanity."

"Then she has read them," Mona said. "Locked drawers never kept out any servant who wanted to snoop." Mona turned her attention to the refreshments set out on the coffee table. "Try the scones with the blackberry jam. We grow the blackberries ourselves."

"No, thank you. I'm not hungry."

Mona could see that Elspeth was very distressed. "I am sorry for your loss, Elspeth."

"It was quite a shock. A natural death is something I could have handled, but someone murdering Beulah—it's unthinkable."

"What do you think happened?"

"Someone outside the farm trespassed and attacked her. Probably a hobo. The railway is not too far from the farm."

"What was Beulah doing outside in the freezing cold at 3 a.m.?"

"I don't know."

"Was it her custom to do so?"

"I don't know. We never talked about such things."

"You said you hired Beulah to help when your mother took ill."

"Yes."

"Was she a trained nurse?"

"I don't know if she was trained as in having a degree, but she was very knowledgeable and a comfort to my mother."

"From what agency did you hire her?"

"You must think me awfully stupid but I don't know. You see, my father hired her. I was still very young at the time."

"Why wasn't she let go after your mother passed away?"

"My father thought I needed a companion, and she was kept on."

"What were her responsibilities?"

"Keep my private rooms straightened, have my wardrobe ready, run errands for me—that type of thing."

"You said she brought you your mail."

"That's right. Always."

"Why was that? Why not the upstairs maid or the butler?"

"I just liked Beulah to bring my mail to me as soon as it came."

"Do you get a lot of mail?"

"Yes, quite a bit. Correspondence with Father's associates, friends, admirers of his work."

"And you."

"Friends."

"Any lovers?"

Elspeth looked aghast. "I had my share of

love letters but I burned them all."

"Why was that?"

"They were unsuitable for a young woman—full of impure suggestions."

"Those impure suggestions can be fun. Ever follow up on one of them?"

"I should say not."

"Did Beulah know about them?"

"She sometimes reads them to me."

Mona frowned. She was tired of getting mixed information from Elspeth. "What can I do for you, Elspeth?"

"I wanted to ask you about what I should tell Sheriff Gideon."

"Like I said—tell him the truth. You hired Mr. Martin on my suggestion to investigate the writer of those letters. Mr. Martin left your employ, and you have no idea where he is. That is the truth, isn't it?"

"If he found anything out, he never told me."

Chloe jumped up on the couch and curled up beside Elspeth.

Mona took notice of Chloe's behavior. She thought the dog an astute judge of humans.

"I have another favor to ask. I will be burying

Beulah in two days. I wondered if you would come to the house for the funeral. I have no other friends, and I don't think I can face it alone."

Mona didn't let on that she thought that a strange statement. After all, Connie would be there. Perhaps it was a testament that Connie and Elspeth were becoming more estranged. "She is being buried on the farm?"

"Yes. Connie has a small cemetery for his employees. So many of them can't afford to purchase a burial plot."

"That's very kind of Connie."

A knock on the door sounded and Thomas peered into the room. "Miss Mona, time for our meeting."

"Thank you, Thomas." Mona rose as did Chloe. "I must go now."

Thomas widened the door, and Samuel appeared with Elspeth's hat and coat.

Elspeth followed Mona and Chloe into the foyer. "Thank you, Mona, for being such a good friend. You will come?"

"Of course. Anything I can do to help."

Mona stood on the portico and waved goodbye, watching Elspeth's car travel down the curving driveway. As soon as the car was out of sight, Mona said to Thomas, "When you get a moment, have the farmhand who washed Mrs. Hopper's car come see me."

Thomas nodded and sent Samuel to find the young man. "Something wrong, Miss Mona?"

"Something is not right with that woman's story."

"She's scared, that's for sure. Never seen a woman whose eyes seem so wide. Can't be normal."

"Yes, but scared of what or of whom?"

"Always start from the person closest to her, I'd say."

Mona grinned. "You wouldn't have happened to go through her coat pockets?"

Thomas drew back. "I should say not, Miss Mona. What kind of talk is that?"

"I'm just pulling your leg."

"No, you're not. Sometimes I think you have the devil in you."

Mona patted Thomas' shoulder. "You pray for me then, Thomas."

"I always pray for you, Miss Mona, but who's

praying for Mrs. Hopper?" He went back inside while Mona remained on the portico. She motioned to a Pinkerton, who was guarding the house.

"Yes, Miss Moon?"

"Have one of your men follow Mrs. Hopper's car to make sure she gets home safely."

"Will do."

"And have him stick with her. I want to see where she goes in the next several days, but instruct him to be discreet. I don't want her to know she's being followed."

The man nodded and motioned to another Pinkerton, who was walking a perimeter check.

Mona hoped she was doing the right thing, but she couldn't shake the notion that Elspeth was lying and possibly in danger.

14

Mona, Dotty, and Violet, dressed in black, stood shivering in the icy wind as they watched Beulah's casket lowered into a grave. Elspeth stood stoically beside Connie as a priest finished his eulogy. The Hopper house staff, standing behind them, looked somewhat aggravated. Sheriff Gideon stood to the side watching everyone.

Mona felt something wet touch her cheek and looked up. It had begun to snow. Inwardly groaning, she cast a glance at Violet, whose cheeks were red from the chill.

Finally, the priest finished and whispered a few words of comfort to Elspeth. Connie dismissed the staff and walked over to Mona. "I hope you can come inside for a few moments, if only to warm up."

"Can you offer us a cup of hot tea?" Mona asked, her hands trembling from the cold.

"I can do better than that. How about a hot toddy?"

"You're on. Lead the way, oh swami."

Mona, Violet, and Dotty locked arms as they trudged over the frost covered pathway toward the Hopper mansion. Mona pulled her coat higher around her neck and wished she had worn a thicker scarf.

When, they reached the mansion, they rushed inside only to be directed to a drawing room warmed by a roaring fire. Connie excused himself, saying Elspeth would be present in a moment. She was still talking to the priest outside.

Violet and Dotty kept their coats on while they stood before the fire rubbing their hands. Mona threw off her coat, hat, and gloves. No one came to collect them.

Dotty asked, "Where did the staff go?"

"They're probably in the kitchen getting warm," Violet said. "Did you notice that some of them didn't have decent coats?"

"It's rather sad," Mona concurred.

"That doesn't happen at Mooncrest Farm," Violet boasted. "Miss Mona bought me two bolts of wool this summer, and I have made four coats with thick linings for our workers."

"I deduct three dollars from a worker's pay for the coat. This covers the cost of the cloth, and Violet volunteers her time to sew them," Mona said. "Workers can also volunteer their time to help other staff members in order to pay back the cost of the cloth. We keep a log book in the equipment barn. People put down their needs in the log and volunteers write when they have finished those jobs."

"I've never heard of such a program," Dotty said, impressed. "Is it working? Be honest, now."

Mona answered, "I don't know, Dotty. That's why I'm assigning you the task of going through the log and double-checking the entries. I need to know if this program is helpful or just wasting everyone's time."

"Oh, good golly," Dotty responded, twisting her lips. This new responsibility meant she would have to travel all over the Bluegrass to check entries listed in the log books, as Mooncrest

Enterprises owned several farms and properties in the area.

"Hello."

Mona, Dotty, and Violet turned around.

Elspeth had changed out of her black widow weed ensemble into a new maroon frock.

Mona went over to Elspeth. "I'm very sorry for your loss."

"Thank you." Elspeth looked at the other two women. "And these are your friends?"

"My friends and also my employees. They are offering to help you."

Elspeth frowned and stepped back. "Help me? In what way?"

Mona motioned to Violet. "Violet is my personal maid. She is also a wiz with a needle and thread. If you have any mending, she can do it right now for you before we leave."

Violet approached Elspeth and did a little curtsey. "If you direct me to where your mending pile and sewing basket are, I can put things to right quickly. I'll be glad to help."

Elspeth said, "That is very nice, but I don't think it is proper."

"Take her offer, Elspeth. Violet is the best

seamstress in the Bluegrass, and this is a one-time offer," Mona encouraged.

"Well, Beulah did some hand-mending for me in her room. I don't know what's there, and a Singer sewing machine is in the laundry room off the kitchen," Elspeth said.

"This is Dotty, my secretary. She can help with your correspondence, if you like," Mona said.

Dotty stepped forward and extended her hand. "How do you do?"

Elspeth looked askance at Dotty. "I guess you can go into my study and put my business and personal mail into two piles. Slice open the envelopes, but don't take the letters out, please. I'll do that." Exasperated, Elspeth pushed back some flyaway hair. "Since Beulah's death, I've gotten behind. What else can you do?"

Dotty dropped her hand, somewhat irritated with the woman's refusal to shake hands. "I know shorthand, take dictation at two hundred words a minute, type a hundred words a minute without error, file, and schedule appointments."

Taking careful note of Elspeth's behavior with Dotty, Mona claimed, "Dotty's a treasure."

"That's awfully kind of you. Yes, I would love your help." She turned to Mona. "You don't mind?"

Mona shook her head. "Dotty will help get things straightened out."

"I can also help find you a personal maid or social secretary if need be," Dotty suggested.

Elspeth said, "You are all so kind. I'm afraid I am at my wit's end. I don't know if I'm coming or going."

"Mrs. Hopper, can you direct me to Miss Beulah's room? I'll start there," Violet said, still standing in her coat.

Elspeth replied, "Just go to the kitchen. The staff will show you the whereabouts of her room and the sewing machine."

Violet made way for the door on the left and Dotty followed, going in search of Elspeth's study.

Once alone, Mona noticed Elspeth was breathing erratically. "Elspeth, are you all right?"

Elspeth put her hand over her chest. "It's this nasty business. The stress has been terrible."

"Shall I call for a doctor?"

"No, please. It will pass." Elspeth said, sitting

near the fire. "Thank you for coming. Connie has not been so sympathetic. I don't think he liked Beulah."

"It's the least I could do under such circumstances."

"Did you see Sheriff Gideon lurking about?"

Mona answered, "He's just doing his job." She paused for a moment. "I noticed your stepson wasn't at the funeral." Since Mona had never seen Wally, she had no idea if he had been present at the funeral or not. She just wanted to see what Elspeth would say.

Elspeth made a snorting noise and looked away. "That one."

"I noticed you had a Catholic priest for the funeral. Beulah wasn't Church of England?"

Elspeth shook her head.

Mona rose. "I can see that you are exhausted, so I'll leave."

"What about your employees?"

"I'll send a car for them in a couple of hours."

Mona grabbed her things and made her way to the foyer.

A blast of chilly air greeted Mona as Elspeth opened the front door. She motioned for Jamison to drive the car to the entrance from where he had parked the Daimler near a grove of naked trees. "I'll be in touch, Elspeth." Mona rushed down the steps to the Daimler. Once inside, she breathed easier. Jamison had kept the car running, and Mona delighted in its toasty warmth. She despised the wintry cold and longed the heat of the desert.

Mona looked out the window at the snow-covered fields, wondering if Elspeth was setting her up to take the fall for Beulah's murder. She just didn't trust the woman.

15

Mona was reviewing a financial report when Samuel reported that Dotty and Violet were home. She nodded and asked him to bring tea and three slices of the chocolate cake with marshmallow icing she had spotted in the kitchen.

Twenty minutes later, Violet knocked on the study door and poked her head inside. "May I?"

"I've been waiting for you."

"Ooh, cake. Yummy." Violet poured herself a cup of tea.

Mona moved from behind her desk to a group of chairs and tables before the marble fireplace.

Dotty hurried into the study with Chloe. "I heard there was cake in here." She spied the cart with the tea and plates of cake. "Nice big pieces, too."

Chloe went over to Mona and whined.

"Where have you been all afternoon?" Mona asked, scratching Chloe behind the ears.

"Chloe came in with us. She was hanging around with some other dogs near the hay barn."

"Disreputable lot," Violet teased.

"We both have a soft spot for bad boys, don't we, Chloe?" Mona cooed.

"This icing is divine," Dotty said, pretending to swoon.

Mona took a bite of her cake. "Oh, gosh, this is good."

All three ladies hurriedly ate their cake and swallowed their tea. Satiated, they lounged before the fire, almost dozing until Mona asked, "What did you find?"

Violet straightened up in her chair. "I think Dotty would agree with me that the house is very disorganized. There is no butler and for a house that size a butler is needed. Mr. Hopper likes to eat at six, but lunch is at one. Very difficult for the kitchen staff, especially when they are short of help. There is no laundress. The maids are expected to clean the entire house, do the laundry, and help in the kitchen when needed. It's too much responsibility for those gals. Most of the staff is young and inexperienced because the older employees have left and found work elsewhere."

"I concur," Dotty said.

"What did you find out about Beulah?" Mona asked Violet.

"I found her room. It was on the second floor, but not near Mrs. Hopper's room. It was down the corridor tucked around a corner."

"When I was in Mrs. Hopper's room on the night of the reception, I saw a door leading to another room."

"That would be Mr. Hopper's connecting bedroom."

Mona said, "Makes sense."

Violet reported, "Beulah's room was very well appointed. She smoked, though. I found European cigarettes in a drawer."

"Maybe that explains why she was out at night. She was smoking," Dotty suggested.

"Why not smoke in your room?" Mona asked.

Violet said, "Maybe smoking is not allowed in the house."

Mona shook her head. "I smelled cigar and cigarette smoke when we were there."

"Come to think of it, I did, too," Violet said.

"What else did you find in Beulah's room?"

"This." Violet reached into her pocket and pulled out a picture. It was photo mounted on cardstock of Elspeth's father, John Alden, and a young girl around the age of thirteen. Mona flipped it over. The words "Paris" and "1907" were written on the back in fading pencil. The distinctive handwriting was tight and jagged.

Mona went over to her desk and pulled out a magnifying glass. She studied the picture in detail.

Violet and Dotty crowded around her.

"Is this Beulah?" Mona asked.

Dotty shrugged. "I never saw the woman."

"Neither had I," Violet volunteered. "Beulah's toiletries and clothes were that of an older woman, though, not someone young, and I saw red hair dye in the bathroom."

"I got the impression Beulah was middle-aged, too." Mona did some quick calculating. "Let's see. If this girl is around twelve or thirteen in 1907, that would make her about forty now, give or take a year or two. Elspeth is in her late twenties and told me she was born when her father was of a later age."

Mona handed the picture to Dotty. "Tell me what you think about this girl."

Dotty took the magnifying glass and studied the picture. "If it weren't for the hair, I would say she resembles Elspeth Hopper very strongly."

"There is no record of John Alden ever being married before Elspeth's mother," Mona said, giving Dotty a knowing look.

"What are you two insinuating?"

"Ah, Violet is using her big high school words," Dotty teased, bumping Violet with her hip.

Violet made a face.

Dotty said, "For goodness sake, Violet, put two and two together! Beulah was John Alden's love child."

Violet's eyes widened. "Oh!" She pulled the photograph out of Dotty's hands and studied it. "I see it now—the resemblance I mean."

"Elspeth told me Beulah was hired to help when her mother became ill," Mona said.

Dotty said, "John Alden could have used that as an excuse to bring his eldest child into the house."

"Surely, Elspeth would have understood who Beulah was," Mona said.

"If she hadn't at first, she would have soon realized that Beulah was her older sister," Dotty said. "They could almost be twins."

"This opens many avenues of speculation," Mona said. "What was their relationship? Did Elspeth get along with Beulah or despise her?"

"Mrs. Hopper seemed distraught at the funeral," Violet said.

Dotty added, "I didn't see any tears, and she didn't seem too upset when I was helping her this afternoon. It was all business."

"Perhaps, she secretly wanted Beulah out of the way," Mona suggested, thinking back on Jellybean's take on the two. Mona remembered him saying that Elspeth relied on Beulah, and Beulah seemed to adore her, but of course, that could have been for show.

"If our guess is right and Beulah is the first-born daughter of John Alden, then she might have resented Elspeth inheriting John Alden's glory, money, and the collection," Dotty said.

"That might have caused serious conflict between the two," Mona said.

"Why didn't she just cut Beulah loose?" Violet asked.

"Perhaps Beulah threatened to go to the newspapers. That's what I would have done," Dotty said.

Mona agreed. "And that stain would have damaged Elspeth's reputation as well as further ruining her father's. Elspeth told me that many archeologists considered John Alden nothing more than a grave robber."

Violet asked, "What do you think, Miss Mona?"

Mona said, "I think John Alden is a king among archeologists. He invented new techniques for researching and cataloging his finds. He was one of the first archeologists to hire a photographer to record his discoveries. Howard Carter of Tutankhamun fame, learned that from him. John Alden's dig of Queen Ahsetsedek's tomb is one of the most scientific of its time. He used men, horses, mules, and camels to remove the debris. It was an amazing accomplishment to find the tomb, let alone excavate it. At that time, everyone was fixated on finding a pharaoh's tomb. No one but John Alden thought a queen's tomb could hold such riches."

"What about his smuggling out the artifacts?" Dotty asked.

"We're talking about a dig that started over fifty years ago and took ten years to finish. I can't speak for John Alden. I don't know the agreement he made with the Ottoman Empire as Egypt was under their jurisdiction at the time, but I know the British Museum underwrote the expedition, which is why they got so many of the artifacts. The laws regarding archeological finds have changed since the late nineteenth century. Alden may have taken what he thought was due to him or promised. Either way, Egypt has not bothered to contest John Alden's will regarding Queen Ahsetsedek, and Elspeth has not confided to me if they have ever approached her with an offer to purchase back some of the artifacts."

"I think Queen Ahsetsedek is somehow behind Beulah's death," Violet said.

"Why?" Mona asked.

"Just a hunch."

Mona hadn't confided to either lady about the threatening letters. She thought Violet's comment interesting because Violet was right so often of the time.

Mona asked, "Dotty, did you find anything?"

"Nothing interesting. Mrs. Hopper's office is a mess. Lots of invitations which have never been answered, but I'm sure they will be rescinded now."

"Are you kidding? The ladies of this community will like nothing more than to get Elspeth in their clutches for the inside scoop," Mona said.

Dotty chuckled.

"Any correspondence from the Chicago or Cincinnati Museum of Art?" Mona asked.

"Nothing that I saw."

"Anything with a return address from out-of-state?"

Dotty shook her head. "I'm going over to the Hopper's tomorrow for a couple of hours. It seems Mrs. Hopper doesn't know how to write a check."

Mona raised an eyebrow. She hardly thought that could be the case, but still wondered. "Just be careful what you say. Your job is to extract information, not give it."

Dotty's face flushed. "I'll be careful. If there is something to find, I'll ferret it out."

Mona gave leave to Dotty and Violet, knowing they must be tired. Violet left to visit her mother, and Dotty went to her house, a small white clapboard, one-bedroom house with blue shutters on the Mooncrest Farm. Mona slipped out through the kitchen with Chloe trailing behind and hurried to see Lord Farley.

She just had to see him!

16

Mona rushed into Lord Farley's arms. "Hold me. Hold me as though you'll never let go."

"Happily," Robert said, cupping his arms around Mona. "Now. Now. What's this about? Look, you've got Chloe upset. Quit whining, Chloe. Your mistress is just having a little nervous breakdown. Tell me all your woes." He led Mona over to a couch.

"I feel so foolish."

"What about?"

"Several minutes ago, I had this overwhelming feeling of dread. It was like I couldn't breathe. The only thing I could think of was to get to you."

Robert pulled Mona close and pressed his cheek against hers. "I know the feeling. You were just experiencing a little whoopsy."

"A whoopsy?"

"It's my made-up word for oops and what-the-hell! It sneaks up on you when you least expect it and then POW! You got a whoopsy. Kind of buckles your knees, doesn't it?"

"Is this what you've been experiencing since the war, Robert? You got the whoopsies?"

"It's why I drank. The whoopsies are not very pleasant."

"No, they're not. I thought I was strong, but—."

"Stop right there. Don't start doubting yourself, Mona. You *are* strong. You've done more for this community in a year than anyone else has in ten. You've given people a chance to finish their schooling, fed people who were hungry, given funding to various charities, kept your employees working with a fair wage. No one has been laid off from Mooncrest Farm or Mooncrest Enterprises since you took over the reins. Do you know what an accomplishment that is during this economic turndown. You've kept families intact. You have really contributed, while I have played the ponies and chased amusement where I can."

"Robert, that's not true. You saved Lady Alice's estate for her, and you've saved my life on more than one occasion."

"And you have saved mine."

"Makes us even, then." Mona leaned against Robert, pondering. "Will we always have the whoopsies? Everything is happening so fast."

"I'm afraid so, my darling, but isn't it nice to lean on someone who understands?"

Chloe leapt upon the couch and snuggled, poking her snout under Mona's hand.

Mona laughed and petted Chloe. "I've got two good friends to save me from the whoopsies."

Robert kissed Mona's forehead. "You gonna marry me, Blondie?"

"I think so."

"When?"

"This time next year we'll be wed."

"I won't disappoint you, Mona. I know you may be my last chance for happiness."

"And you, mine."

Mona and Robert wrapped their arms around each other and just as their kissing became heated, the housekeeper appeared with a tray of coffee. Chloe growled as Robert chuckled when he noticed Mona blushing. "If you would let me announce our engagement, then people catching us snogging wouldn't find it so risqué."

"Don't your servants knock before entering, and please quit using that word snogging? It sounds like a noise a pig would make."

Robert grinned and snorted, much to Mona's dismay. "Come on. Have some coffee. You look like you need something hot, and you can tell me what happened." Robert poured a cup for Mona which she accepted gratefully.

"I had gone to Beulah Bradley's funeral and left Violet and Dotty with Elspeth to help."

"You mean to snoop."

"Well, yes, if you want to put it that way."

"I think you should stay away from Elspeth Hopper. Something's not right there, old girl."

"My instinct says so, too, but why, I ask myself? I wish I had never gone upstairs during Elspeth's reception and found her weeping."

"You would have gotten suckered into her tale of woe somehow."

"Listen to this. Violet found a photograph of Beulah with John Alden around 1907." Mona pulled the picture out of her pocket and handed it over.

Robert laughed. "Now you are stealing photos. Oh, dear."

"Take a look at it."

Robert held the photo up and studied it.

"What do you think?"

"So, this is Beulah. How old do you think she is in this picture? Fifteen, perhaps? She's at that gawky stage." He turned over the photograph and read the writing. "I think it is odd that John Alden knew Beulah before Elspeth was even born. They are standing very close to each other, smiling, almost touching. Beulah is wearing very expensive clothes—not the kind a servant could afford."

"Look at the beading on her dress. That had to be hand-stitched. It was expensive then and still is today. If you didn't know the people, what would you say their relationship was?"

"The girl is a relative of the man's—a niece or a daughter." Robert looked up at Mona. "John Alden didn't marry until late in his life, so it isn't surprising that he had a baby born on the wrong side of the blanket. At least, it looks like he supported her. Many men walk away from such responsibilities."

Robert handed back the photograph. "You think Beulah was murdered because she was John Alden's daughter?"

"No, I think she was killed because she was blackmailing someone about being John Alden's daughter."

Robert shook his head. "Who would care? This type of scandal would finish a man's career and reputation in the last century, but with all the bed-hopping and divorces movie stars do nowadays, society is more relaxed about such things."

"I don't believe society is as freethinking about such matters as you think. I told Sheriff Gideon that we were together much of the night Beulah was murdered. He seemed shocked."

Frowning, Robert said, "Be careful there, Mona. I've made some inquiries about Sheriff Gideon. He is a foot-washing Baptist who believes in the strict interpretation of the Bible. He is known to be fanatical about 'wrong doers' and is not averse to using his fists to get a confession."

"That's what Jellybean was referring to and why he wanted to get out of town."

"Sheriff Gideon will automatically have a grudge against you for just being who you are."

"In what way?"

"He doesn't believe women should have a public face, and to make matters worse, the bank with which you do business foreclosed on his family farm several years ago. If he thinks you are a Jezebel to boot, you will make the fur on his back stand up. He might want to make you pay for your 'sins.'"

"Will he think the same way about you?"

"Of course not. I'm a man."

"I don't know how men think the same rules should not apply to their gender."

"I don't make the rules, luv, but there it is." Robert took a sip of his coffee. "Let's get back to Beulah. Whom do you think she was blackmailing?"

"Elspeth would be my first choice."

"Stabbing is very personal and full of rage. A person also has to be strong to stab someone. Don't women usually use a gun or poison to kill?"

"A gun would have been too loud."

"And why outside in the cold?" Robert

snapped his fingers. "The murderer must have left footprints in the snow. Too bad we don't have access to the Sheriff Gideon's report."

Mona proposed, "Let's look at this logically. If I were a petite woman like Elspeth, how would I kill someone heavier and taller like Beulah?"

"How about a tumble down the staircase?"

"Easy enough to push someone even for Elspeth, but there's always the chance the victim wouldn't break their neck, so that's too iffy."

"Car accident?"

"Elspeth would have to be driving the car to create an accident. I don't think she drives, and she wouldn't have the faintest idea how to mechanically sabotage a car."

"How would you know what Elspeth can and cannot do? She lived for years in Egypt. She's extremely educated. I bet she's not as helpless as she makes out. She might be playing you. Stabbing is a quiet and efficient way to kill someone. Let's be firm about this. Whoever stabbed Beulah planned it or why else bring the knife along?"

"You're probably right. I am making too many assumptions. What I need are facts."

"Jellybean said Beulah's body was found with

the knife sticking out of her back. What he did not relay was how many times Beulah had been stabbed. Was it once or several times? Did the knife puncture the heart? Stabbing from the back requires knowledge of the anatomy because of the rib cage. It's easier to kill someone from the front. From the back, you have to know right where to stab."

"Jellybean probably didn't know. We're not even sure he saw the body. Perhaps that's what he had been told."

Robert put his cup down. "You can theorize all you want, Mona, but without information, you are dead in the water, so to speak."

"Ha ha."

"Seriously, let this go. It's none of your concern, and the more you meddle, the more you draw Sheriff Gideon's attention to yourself."

"You're right, Robert. I'll be supportive to Elspeth but I'll quit sleuthing. I'm done with it," Mona said, not foreseeing events had already been put in motion which would spill over into her life soon.

17

Mona hurried to change. Dexter and Willie were coming for dinner. She still was not used to dressing formally just to eat her evening meal, but standards had to be upheld. The servants expected it.

Since Violet had the night off, Mona was left to her own devices for selecting her attire. She chose a dove gray, chiffon gown with cranes flying upward on the bottom panel of the dress. It was one of her favorite dresses. It was elegant without being fussy and one of her most comfortable gowns. Mona threw the dress on and didn't bother with stockings. She knew Violet would be horrified if she knew. What did it matter? No one was going to see her legs anyway. Checking her makeup and hair, Mona gave a last glimpse in the vanity mirror before dabbing on a bit of perfume and stepping into gray suede dress heels.

There was a knock on the door. "Come in."

Dora, the downstairs maid, poked her head in, knowing she was not to enter the room. "Miss Mona, the Deatheridges are here."

"Thank you. Show them into the drawing room."

"I've already done so, and Mr. Deatheridge has gone ahead and mixed martinis."

Mona frowned. "Of course, he has. Thank you, Dora. I'll be down in a moment."

Dora smiled and closed the bedroom door.

Mona waited to ensure that Dora had gone downstairs before she exited the room and locked the bedroom door, tucking the key in her brassiere. Only Violet and Mona had access to Mona's private rooms because Mona insisted that her bedroom be off limits to everyone but the two of them.

She soon joined Dexter and Wilhelmina in the drawing room just as Dexter was pouring a liquid concoction into martini glasses. "Hello, you two." Mona went over and kissed Willie on the cheek almost spilling the drink she had in hand. "Oh, gosh, so sorry."

"Don't worry, honey. Nothing valuable in this glass. I'm drinking a soda water. How dull my life has become."

Dexter said, "Now, darling, don't complain."

Willie grumbled, "I don't know why everyone thinks I'm turning into an alcoholic. I resent the implication."

"Now, darling, I never said you were an alcoholic. I said you needed to taper off a bit." Dexter handed a glass to Mona which she waved off.

"No thank you, Dexter. Robert is joining us for dinner. He's trying not to drink, so I don't want to put temptation in his way. You both understand."

"Of course we do, dear." Willie thought for a moment. "Does that mean we won't be having wine with dinner?"

Mona chuckled. "I'm afraid so, but Chef Bisaillon had concocted some wonderful non-alcoholic beverages for our dinner tonight."

Willie made a face. "Oh, Lordy, what horrible swill is he going to make us drink? I hope whatever it is, it isn't sweet."

"Well, I better get rid of this stuff before Robert gets here." Dexter tilted back his head and swallowed his martini in two gulps and then did the same with Mona's glass. Seeing the astonished looks on both Mona's and Willie's faces, he said, "Good gin and vermouth should never go to waste."

"I hope you'll be able to stagger to the dining table, Dexter," Mona said.

"I am known for holding my liquor, Madame."

"We shall see."

"Hello, everyone," Robert said, striding into the room. He came over to Mona and gave her a quick peck on the lips and then kissed Willie on the cheek.

Dexter quickly hid the martini glasses and went over to shake Robert's hand. "Good to see you, Robert."

Robert kidded, "Oh, yes, it's been so long. Yesterday, wasn't it?"

Curious, Mona asked, "Where did you two meet up?"

"Let us men have our little secrets," Dexter said.

Willie made a face. "Well, now I'm intrigued."

"It was nothing, really. Just bumped into Dexter outside the bank."

"Speaking of the bank, how's that deal coming along?" Mona asked.

"You've got it. All you have to do is sign the papers which I have brought along with me."

"What's this?" Robert asked, looking between Mona and Dexter.

"I've bought a bank," Mona announced.

"Do you think that's wise, Mona, considering the state of the economy?" Robert asked, pouring himself a club soda with ice.

"I didn't like the way I was treated, so I purchased the bank. I want to make it female friendly."

"Quite so," Willie added, holding up her glass in agreement.

"And banks aren't welcoming to the gentler sex?" Robert asked.

"No, they are not. It's hard to get a loan if you're a woman and if you're married, every bank transaction has to be approved by the husband. Now, that's not right. Look at what you had to do for Lady Alice. You had to go to the bank and pitch for her to get a loan, and Alice is an aristocrat. Imagine what it is like for a normal woman to do business with a bank."

"Good luck, my dear. I hope there's not another run on banks like there was in 1932."

"I'll cross my fingers," Mona said, smiling. "I know there is a great risk."

"Can we please talk about something else other than business?" Willie asked, pouting.

"I have some pleasant news," Robert offered. "Will Rogers is coming to Cincinnati later this month, and I bought four tickets. I thought the four of us could go and make a weekend of it."

"I would love to see the glass mosaics in Union Terminal again," Mona said.

"Could we go to the Cincinnati Art Museum?" Willie asked. "Could we?"

"That seems a splendid idea, Robert, as long as the roads are passable this time of the year," Dexter said.

"We'll go by train," Mona said. "I'll make reservations at the Netherland tomorrow for the four of us. It will be such fun."

Willie gushed, "The Netherland is so elegant. Remember, Mona. It's where I first met you, and you were wearing that risqué, gold lamé gown. Every man had his eyes on you."

Mona smiled. "It was the first nice evening gown I'd ever owned, but it was a satin, slipper gown."

"Hmm, I remember a gold lamé dress and it was backless."

"Yes, it was. I still have it."

"Perhaps you will wear it for an encore at the Netherland?" Robert asked, his eyes flashing at Mona.

"If it will please you."

"It would."

"I have some interesting news myself," Willie announced. "You'll never know who I saw today."

"Who, darling?" Dexter said, sitting down next to her.

"I was driving on Water Street when I saw Jack Keene. I pulled over because I wanted to ask him if the rumor was true."

"What rumor is that?" Mona asked.

"I've heard through the grapevine that he has thrown his hat into the ring and wants the Racing Commission to buy his farm for the new race-track."

"It will never happen," Robert said. "They are looking at five other locations and Jack is asking too much money for his property."

"But, Robert, there is already a racecourse on the property, and there is that limestone building which could be turned into a clubhouse," Willie said. "That will knock costs down considerably for the new racetrack."

"I think it is a toss up," Dexter said. "Jack's place is too far out of town. They'll build another racetrack in town so they can get the foot traffic. Otherwise, people will have to have a car to get out there."

"They'll have transportation from town to the track if they pick Jack's place," Willie said. "Trolleys or something like that."

"Did Jack Keene tell you?" Mona asked.

"I didn't get to ask him. I pulled the car over and called out to him when I saw he was walking with someone."

"Who was it? Don't hold us in suspense," Dexter pleaded.

"Consuelo Hopper."

"Consuelo! What's she doing back?" Dexter said, obviously flustered.

"Are you sure it was Consuelo?" Mona asked.

"I'm positive."

Before any more questions could be asked, there was a knock on the door and Samuel slipped in and made his way to Mona, whispering in her ear.

"Thank you, Samuel. Tell Burl to let him in."

"Yes, Miss Mona." Samuel turned and left the room.

"What was that all about?" Willie asked.

"Sheriff Gideon is at my front gate desiring admittance."

Dexter sputtered, "Whatever for?"

"At this late hour. It's after eight o'clock. The man should be home having dinner with his wife," Robert said.

"It's a good thing you're here, Dexter. Something tells me this is not a social call."

"Let's go into the library, Mona," Dexter said. "You two stay here."

"I want to be present," Robert insisted.

Dexter held up his hand. "I'll call for you if I need to, but for now, stay put with Wilhelmina. Please."

As Mona and Dexter proceeded to the library,

they heard a car pull up before the entrance to Moon Manor.

Dexter called to Samuel in readiness by the front door. "Hold the Sheriff at bay for a few minutes until we get settled and then bring up a pot of coffee with three cups and something sweet to eat, Samuel. We want to appear social."

"Yes, sir," Samuel said, nodding. He, too, was concerned. A visit from any lawman was never a good thing in his book.

Mona asked, "Do you know what this is about, Dexter?"

"No, but you're right. This isn't a social call. Best get ready. This might get rocky."

The sense of dread that Mona had been feeling dissipated. Like a bull in the ring, she was going to lower her head and trample over anything that threatened her. Mona gave Dexter a steely look. "Bring it on. I'm ready."

And Mona was.

18

Mona sat behind her mammoth desk in the library while Dexter sat in one of the two chairs placed before the desk. "Sheriff Gideon, what an unexpected pleasure. You know my lawyer, Dexter Deatherage."

Gideon nodded. "How do you do."

Dexter rose and shook hands with the Sheriff. "Likewise."

"Please be seated, gentlemen."

If Gideon was startled by the sight of Dexter, he didn't show it. "Thank you, ma'am."

"It's miss, still."

"I noticed Lord Farley's roadster outside. Odd choice for winter."

Mona didn't reply. She knew the Sheriff was baiting her. "He's here. We were about to sit for dinner. How may I help you?"

"I'm sorry if I spoiled your dinner plans, Miss Moon, but this is an official call."

"Oh? In what way?"

"The law caught up with Jellybean Martin in Detroit. He is being escorted back to Lexington for questioning in the murder of Beulah Bradley."

Dexter asked, "What possible motive would Jellybean Martin have to kill Beulah Bradley?"

Sheriff Gideon turned toward Dexter. "You know this Jellybean?"

"Of course, everyone in my line of work knows Jellybean. We use him frequently. He's a private detective."

"A black man as a detective. Don't that beat all."

Neither Mona or Dexter responded. They both realized Gideon was trying to get a rise out of them.

Gideon turned his attention back to Mona. "I asked you if you knew this Jellybean fellow, and I don't think you were quite truthful with me."

"Yes, I admit I was evasive. I don't know you, Sheriff, and this concerned a private matter with Elspeth Hopper. I felt it was her story to tell you if she wanted."

"Well, ma'am, I mean miss, it doesn't work like that in a murder investigation. When I ask you a question, you must speak the truth, like your hand is on the Bible swearing an oath."

"There's the truth and there are facts that appear to be the truth," Mona replied.

"Sounds like you are talking gobbledygook. There's the truth and that's it. Now, I'm gonna ask you again—do you know Jellybean Martin?"

"Why do you think I would know this Jellybean?" Mona asked.

"When I informed you at the bank that a Beulah Bradley had been murdered, you didn't seem surprised. In fact, you didn't ask who Beulah Bradley was. That implies you already knew. Maybe this Jellybean had already reported the murder to you?"

"I'll do better in the future to act shocked when I hear bad news."

"I'm only gonna ask you one more time. Do you know Jellybean Martin?"

Mona looked at Dexter, who nodded slightly. "Yes."

"How well?"

"I have hired him on occasions."

"Why?"

"Because he can ferret out information a white detective can't."

"Fair enough." Gideon scratched his ear. "Did you recommend him to Elspeth Hopper?"

"I did."

"Why?"

"Someone sent threatening letters to her, and Mrs. Hopper felt someone close to her might be sending those letters."

"Did Mrs. Hopper say she felt Beulah Bradley was sending those letters?"

"No."

"Did she say who she thought was sending them?"

"No."

"Why not? You said she thought someone close might be sending them."

"She had received uncomplimentary letters before, but felt these letters were different. I get threatening letters myself. Mr. Deatherage files them away if he thinks they are harmless or has the Pinkertons investigate the sender if he takes a letter more seriously."

"Why did these letters seem different to Mrs. Hopper?"

Dexter cut in. "Sheriff, you know that Miss Moon can't answer these types of questions. It's considered secondhand information. You need to ask Mrs. Hopper."

"I did ask Mrs. Hopper. Now I want to see if what she told me fits what she told Miss Moon." Gideon faced Mona. "I know you had several private conversations with her, and she pleaded for your help. Now I'll ask again—why does Mrs. Hopper think these letters are different?"

"The letters that formed the messages were cut out from magazines and pasted. She had never received such letters before, and the postmarks of the letters followed her as she traveled to Lexington."

"I still don't understand why Jellybean is so important. Surely the rest of the kitchen staff can answer your questions," Dexter said.

"Their fingerprints weren't found on the knife sticking out of Miss Bradley's back."

Dexter didn't show any emotion when he asked, "Are you saying Jellybean's were?"

"Yes."

"That's easy to explain. He worked in the kitchen," Mona said.

"Only Jellybean's prints were found on the knife. No one else's."

Mona shot Dexter a worried glance and then asked the Sheriff, "So you think he is the murderer?"

Gideon replied, "Didn't say that. Just said I wanted to talk with him."

"I don't understand," Mona said.

"Beulah Bradley died from a knife wound, but she suffered from arsenic poisoning."

"What!" Dexter exclaimed.

Mona asked, "What has led the coroner to that conclusion? Did he notice Aldrich-Mees lines on her fingernails?"

"Funny you should know about that, Miss Moon, but yes, the doc noticed the white lines across Miss Bradley's fingernails."

"I bet that is why Beulah didn't eat with the staff and had her meals alone. She also prepared her own meals. She must have been suspicious."

"Who told you that?"

"Jellybean Martin."

"Now, you see why it is important I speak

with this Jellybean."

Mona said, "He won't cooperate if you threaten him with violence."

"I use standard interrogation techniques taught by law enforcement."

"That's what I'm afraid of." Mona and Gideon glared at each other in a standoff.

Dexter handed Sheriff Gideon a business card. "I'll be representing Jellybean Martin, so you can interview him only in my presence. This is my contact information. He's coming in on the train?"

"He'll be here around four at the Lexington train depot. I'm to pick him up."

"I'll be there, and I expect to confer with my client before you interrogate him."

"Is that all, Sheriff? Our dinner is waiting," Mona said.

"Just a few more questions, please."

"Shoot," Mona said.

"What contact has either of you had with Cadwallader or Consuelo Hopper?"

"I've never met either of them," Mona said.

"You, Mr. Deatherage?"

"I haven't seen Wally since he got back to

town, but I understand Consuelo is here, too."

"Have you seen her?"

"No, but my wife did today. She was telling us about it when you arrived."

"What is your relationship with Cadwallader or Consuelo Hopper?"

"I don't have much to do with Wally. I don't like him, and he doesn't like me. As for Consuelo, I used to be engaged to her, but you already knew that."

Sheriff Gideon smiled and rose. "Thank you for your time."

"Won't you stay for dinner?" Mona asked.

"That's right kind of you, but my wife is waiting for me."

At that moment there was a knock at the door. Samuel and Obadiah carried in two trays—one with coffee and the other with slices of angel food cake with lemon icing.

"That sure looks tempting," Sheriff Gideon said, glancing longingly at the cake.

"Samuel, wrap up this cake for the Sheriff. He's leaving."

"No, Miss Moon. Can't take it. Might look like a bribe."

"Oh, for goodness sake, Sheriff. Didn't you say your wife had been sick? Take it home for her. I don't know anyone who can resist my chef's angel food cake."

Gideon flipped his Stetson around and around in his hands, thinking. "Since you say it's for my wife, I'll be much obliged then. She hasn't had a treat in a long while."

"Samuel, wrap up the rest of the cake too. Take it to Sheriff Gideon's car. Thank you, Obadiah. That is all."

"Shall I remove the coffee, too, Miss?" Obadiah asked.

"Yes, thank you. We are finished." Rising, Mona said to Sheriff Gideon, "Let me walk you out."

As they walked toward the front door, Sheriff Gideon looked about the rich furnishings and artwork. "I understand you weren't born to all of this."

"No, I worked as a cartographer before. I'm from New York City—a transplanted Yankee."

Sheriff Gideon smiled. "I was born and raised here. It's all I know."

"Yes," Mona said in response, not knowing

what else to say.

"I gotta ask you something."

"Really, Sheriff, enough is enough," Mona said, irritated.

"This has nothing to do with the case. It's something I heard."

Resigned, Mona said, "Ask away, but hurry. My guests are waiting."

"People tell me that you pay black folk the same amount as white men."

"I pay for a job well done. I don't care who does it as long as they're good at their work."

"So it is true, then."

Mona didn't respond.

"It's making a lot of people angry—you treating blacks the same as whites."

"People like you?"

"Just saying."

"Are you threatening me, Sheriff Gideon?"

"No, ma'am. I'm advising you. People don't take kindly to changes, especially from an outsider."

"Noted. Tell your wife I wish her a speedy recovery." Mona opened the front door.

Sheriff Gideon put on his cowboy hat and

exited Moon Manor.

Mona closed the door and went back to the drawing room, thinking the entire interview had been a fishing expedition.

What was Gideon after?

19

A few days later a blizzard hit the Bluegrass. Everything was blue and white—brilliant blue sky and startling white below. The only other color was brown—that of bare trees either standing or fallen across the frozen countryside.

Mona got a call from Jack Keene's secretary. Mr. Keene was having a skating party at his home, and she was invited. Mona readily accepted, interested in seeing the farm Jack Keene wanted to sell for the new racetrack. After hanging up, she called Robert, who had gotten a call, too, and replied, "We better hurry. The roads will be bad, and it will take a long time to get to Jack's house."

Thirty minutes later, Jamison picked Mona and Robert up in a truck with a chainsaw in the back. The roads were icy and covered with debris from the storm, and more than once, Jamison and Robert had to remove broken tree limbs from the road. It took over an hour to arrive at Jack Keene's ancestral home—Keene Place. The grand mansion, built in 1800, stood on a hill overlooking Versailles Pike.

Jamison drove up the driveway, letting Mona and Robert off at the front main double doors. Waving goodbye, Jamison put the stick shift in first and made way to park among the other vehicles on the country lane down below the house.

Many people, dressed in snow suits or skiing outfits, were mingling and sipping bourbon toddies outside the front of the house before a bonfire. Mona and Robert greeted people they knew before entering into the impressive white mansion that blended with the soft falling snow.

"Why two separate front doors?" Mona whispered to Robert, taking off her gloves in the hallway.

"It had to do with boots and mud."

"In what way?"

"One side led to the office and gentlemen's

quarters. Men could enter the house during working hours without taking off their muddy boots to do paperwork. The other side was considered the social part of the house, and people were expected to enter with clean shoes as to keep those quarters clean. Made less work for the servants."

"Slaves, you mean."

"Let's not start the Civil War again. That history is long behind the South."

"I'll behave."

"Lord Farley! So nice of you to come." A nice-looking, middle-aged man hailed from the top of the staircase. He rushed down the stairs and extending his hand, shook Robert's heartily.

"Hello. Mona, may I introduce John Keene, our host."

John lifted Mona's hand and kissed it. "Enchanté."

"Nice to meet you, Mr. Keene."

"What's this Mr. Keene? Call me Jack. Everyone does. We've met before, Miss Moon."

"Call me Mona, please. Where have we met?"

"It was at a derby party last spring. You were wearing a black and white ensemble without the proper undergarments. That dress caused quite a sensation in our little backwater community, I must say."

"They say clothes make the man—or the woman. What did you think of that dress, Jack?"

Jack's eyes danced. "I think the less clothes a woman has on, the better." He elbowed Robert. "Eh, Lord Farley."

Mona laughed. Jack Keene was obviously a sybarite, a refreshing change from all the buttoned-up Puritans she had been meeting for the past year.

"Listen, kids, you can wander anywhere you want in the house. A buffet with finger food is set out in the dining room, but most people are heading over to the clubhouse. There's a big pot of burgoo over there to take the chill off."

"Clubhouse?" Mona asked.

"That's what I call it. I'm hoping the farm is bought for the racetrack and they use the building as a clubhouse. You can't miss it. That's where we're having sled-riding, and there's also skating at the pond if you brought skates." Jack turned at the sound of a truck pulling up. "Oh, just in time. One of my men has just driven up. We're having a shuttle today. He will take you directly to the clubhouse."

Grinning, Robert turned to Mona. "Well?"

"I've never been sledding," Mona explained to Jack. "I grew up in New York City."

"Say no more," Jack said. "You kids have fun. Stop back in before you leave for home."

Mona and Robert hurried outside and climbed into the back of the truck with other revelers. Everyone's mood was gay until the brisk wind, caused by the moving truck, cut across their faces. Mona put her gloved hands over her face while Robert blocked the wind with his back.

Mercifully, the ride was a short one. Robert jumped from the back of the truck and helped the women down onto the ground. Mona was the last passenger to disembark from the truck bed.

"Your cheeks are as bright as cherries," Robert commented. "Let's go inside and get something to eat. It will warm you up."

"That wind was something," Mona replied. She looked at the crowd of people sledding down a nearby hill, which was crowded with excited children, barking dogs, and laughing adults using sleds of all types including large pieces of cardboard. "Oh, Robert, let me try first. I've never been on a sled."

"Okay, if you wish." Robert and Mona both found cardboard lying on the ground and, following the example of younger folk, pushed off only to make it halfway down the hill before they sank into the powdery snow.

Laughing, Mona picked up her soggy cardboard and called out to Robert, "This is no good. We need a real sled to carry our weight."

"Let's see if we can borrow someone's," Robert said, trudging up the hill. He grabbed Mona's hand, pulling her along.

When Robert reached the top, a whiskey flask was thrust into his face. "Looks like you might need this, Lord Farley."

Robert pushed a man's arm away from his face. "No, thank you, Wally."

"I heard you had become a teetotaler. Who's this lovely lady with hair as white as snow accompanying you?"

"Mona, may I present Cadwallader Hopper to you. Wally, this is Madeline Mona Moon."

"So this is the niece to whom crazy Manfred left all the Moon money. Oh, I bet your Aunt

Melanie didn't like that one bit—not one bit."

"How do you do, Mr. Hopper," Mona said, trying to show that Wally gave her the creeps. Maybe it was due to his overly-pomaded hair or his sticky-looking mustache that wiggled like a caterpillar under his nose—or perhaps it was due to the fact that Wally was blotto and stank like cheap booze.

Wally called over his shoulder. "Auntie, come quick. Meet the new mistress of Moon Manor."

A stunning blonde woman with steel gray eyes and dressed in the latest European snow bunny outfit strode over. "I am Consuelo Hopper. Whom am I addressing?"

"So sorry, Auntie. This strapping hunk of a man is Lord Farley."

Consuelo nodded. "I am acquainted with your father, Lord Farley. I attended a weekend house party at your ancestral estate several years ago. Your father and I still exchange Christmas cards."

"And this yellow-eyed wench is Mona Moon, the new mistress of all that is Moon," Wally said, rocking on his heels.

Mona secretly wished that Wally would fall on his backside into the snow and pass out, but she smiled and said, "Nice to meet you, Miss Hopper."

"I understand you are a friend of my sister-in-law's."

"I've tried to be helpful. I know what it is like to be in new surroundings and amongst new people."

"Don't you think Elspeth is a bit neurotic and a waste of your time?"

"I don't know what you mean."

Consuelo shrugged, "Well, I see that you are a loyal friend."

"As a sister-in-law should be as well."

Wally burst out laughing. "She's got you there, Consuelo."

Undeterred, Consuelo pressed on, "I didn't know you were a friend of Jack's—being so new to the area yourself."

"Excuse us," Robert said, trying to hide his anger at the Hoppers' rudeness. "We are going to borrow a sled. Mona's never been sledding before."

"Take ours then. We're finished," Consuelo said.

Wally grinned as he handed over the reins of

two wooden sleds. "It's better to lie on your stomach going down and steer with your hands. The oak trees at the bottom of the hill are to be avoided at all costs. We wouldn't want an Ethan Frome incident, would we?"

"Chin chin," Consuelo said, walking away.

Wally grinned at Mona before running to catch up with his aunt.

Mona turned to Robert. "Dexter was in love with that harridan?"

"No accounting for taste. Let's forget them. Are you still willing to try?" Robert jiggled the rope reins of the sleds.

"Yes, you go down first, so I can see how it is done."

"See these wooden pieces?"

"Yes."

"It's just like riding a horse. Pull on the left lever to go left. Pull on the right lever to go right."

"Seems simple enough. You go first and then I'll follow."

"Okay. You can sit up and steer with your feet or lie down on your stomach. And watch out for those trees. Wally wasn't kidding about them being dangerous. See how everyone is going to the left of them?"

Mona observed how the sleds were maneuvering either to the left or to the right of a copse of trees, many of them landing in the flowing spring beyond. "Go on. I'll be right behind you."

Determined to have some fun and forget about the Hoppers, Mona lay down on the sled and kicked off with her feet. Within seconds she was flying down the steep hill, laughing until she discovered the levers didn't work. Frantically, pulling on either lever, she looked up and discovered she was heading straight for a massive tree trunk. Mona rolled off the sled only to send it flying into a tree to be smashed into pieces.

Several of the sledders rushed over and helped Mona to her feet. Brushing the snow from her clothes, Mona glanced up the hill and saw Consuelo and Wally watching. Seeing that she wasn't injured, they moseyed over to the club-house.

"Mona! Mona! Are you hurt?" Robert asked, rushing over.

"Just my pride."

"What happened?"

"The levers didn't work. I couldn't steer the sled."

Robert's brow furrowed as he scanned for Wally and Consuelo in the crowd. "Those jerks. I'm gonna find Wally and beat him to a pulp."

Mona placed her hand on Robert's arm. "Don't spoil the party for everyone."

"No one would blame me for beating the tar out of Wally. No one can stand him."

"There are children here. Don't start a brawl."

"Want to go home?"

"Goodness no! I want another sled—one that works. Except for the end, it was fun. Please, let's sled some more."

"Okay, you're the boss, my lady love."

Robert found an abandoned sled, and they sledded together for another hour until Mona complained she couldn't feel her fingers anymore due to the cold. They rushed to the clubhouse where they ate large bowls of burgoo and drank cups of hot apple cider, celebrating the afternoon with casual friends.

On their way out, Wally and Consuelo stopped by Robert and Mona's table. "I saw you had trouble with one of our sleds," Wally said.

"Not really," Mona replied, buttering a roll.

Consuelo added, "I should have mentioned the broken levers. I'm so sorry. I simply forgot."

"It's forgotten."

"I wouldn't want you to think I placed you at risk on purpose."

Mona looked up at Consuelo and laughed. "Oh, my goodness. You are such a drama queen! If you think your silly threats bother me, you are barking up the wrong tree. My own aunt thought she could take me down, and she ended up thrown out of Moon Enterprises and living on a pittance which I dole out. Now scoot, both of you, before I get angry."

Bristling, Consuelo said, "No one talks to me that way."

"I just did. What are you going to do about it?"

"You'll see."

"Go play with the other kiddies. You bore me."

Consuelo raised her hand as though to strike Mona, but Wally pulled her away.

"What the hell was that about?" Robert asked, watching them leave.

"Consuelo was trying to warn me off from Elspeth. I would say that woman usually gets her way and doesn't like to be contradicted. I'll think I'll pay a visit to Aunt Melanie tomorrow. Maybe she can enlighten me on Consuelo Hopper."

"Forget her. Let's head out. It will be dark in a couple of hours, and I want to be off the roads by then."

"Yes, let's go, but be careful, Robert. This isn't the end of Consuelo Hopper. That woman has a mean streak in her, and today has been just a taste. I want to find out why Consuelo ran off to live in Venice. I think Aunt Melanie might know."

Mona followed Robert from the clubhouse to the truck. The day had heated up turning the powdery snow into slush. They climbed into the front with Jamison, who pulled out as soon as Robert closed the door.

Mona was glad to be going home. Tomorrow was going to be a big day. She hadn't seen her Aunt Melanie for over a month and didn't relish the thought of visiting her, but if anyone knew about Consuelo Hopper, it would be Melanie.

Or least, Mona hoped so.

20

"This is an unexpected turn of events. Most unpleasant I must say. Here to eat crow?" Melanie said, lounging on a couch.

Mona took a seat opposite her.

"Most people wait to be asked to be seated," Melanie spat out.

"Not if they own the furniture, which I do. Enough of this posturing."

"Heard about your almost sledding mishap. I can see it, too. Your face looks very rough from being outdoors."

"Funny that bit of gossip should have made its way to you so quickly."

"I still have friends in this town, Mona."

"As you say."

Melanie guffawed. "So it is true, then. When

are your reflexes going to dull? It would have been nice for you to crash into the tree, and the Moons be rid of you at last."

"The feeling is quite mutual, dear Auntie, but I'm not here to spar with you. I want information, which I'm willing to pay for, so let's make a deal."

Melanie's expression changed from that of an indulgent cat to one of a predatory panther. She sat up and took notice. "What are you offering?"

"A thousand dollars for all you know about the Hopper family—especially Wally or Consuelo. Five hundred more if the information checks out with my detectives, and another five hundred more deposited in the bank of your choice for your two children if all of you have no contact with the Hoppers. In addition, you are to tell my men if anyone in the Hopper family tries to contact you or your children. That includes letters, phone calls, telegrams, or smoke signals from a mountain top."

"My, my. That's a mouthful." Melanie stared, trying to gauge Mona's desperation. "I want my seat back on the Moon Enterprise board."

"No deal. Take what I'm offering."

Melanie hesitated.

Mona grabbed her purse and rose.

"Okay. Okay. You win. I can't turn down the money—not after the tuppence you give me to live on."

"Let me remind you that you have more discretionary income than ninety percent of the country, and yet, you give nothing back to the community."

"Sticks and stones, Mona. Sticks and stones."

Mona studied her aunt. They looked similar in so many ways. They both had traits of albinism, although Melanie's hair was not quite so pale with a tint of ashen blonde. While Mona's eyes were yellow, Melanie's were light, almost silvery in certain light. Neither had pinkish eyes as a true albino might have, but both were very light-skinned and had to be careful in sunlight. Mona could not deny that Melanie was a beautiful woman with an exquisite, ethereal appearance, but her admiration stopped there.

"Do we have a deal, Melanie?"

Melanie breathed out a reluctant, "Yes."

"Good." Mona pulled out a contract and a fountain pen. "Sign here."

Melanie's mouth dropped open. "Can't a handshake work? We are family."

Mona chuckled. "That's precisely why I'm getting this in writing. Put your John Hancock right there."

Sighing, Melanie signed the contract.

"Now spill."

"When will I get my money?"

"As soon as the Pinkertons investigate your stories, and Melanie, don't hold back. If you come up with nothing more than gossip, the deal is off."

"But that's all I have. I was a child during many of these stories and know them because I overheard my parents talking." Melanie pursed her lips while crossing her legs. "Very well. A deal's a deal. I wasn't very close to Consuelo or Cornelius, but Wally and I ran around in the same circles somewhat."

"Tell me about the family. What do people say about the Hoppers behind their backs?"

"The Hoppers put on a respectable facade, but of course, gambling addiction runs through the family. That's how they lost their money. Old man Hopper just couldn't stay away from the racetracks, and what's worse, he'd bet against his own horses."

"That's Connie's father?"

"Yes, the trouble started with him. He inherited his mother's predilections, you see."

"Connie's grandmother?"

"People said she was barmy."

"Like insane?"

"Like Jane Eyre crazy. You know the type of crazy that requires leather restraints and padded rooms."

"Go on."

"It was supposed to be this big secret, but everyone knew."

"What else," Mona encouraged.

"Madness runs in the family, dear girl. Why else would they shuffle old Consuelo off to Venice? To get rid of her, of course. She never understood Southern feminine decorum, and with that temper of hers, nasty things were always happening."

"Give me an example."

"Let me think. I was at a party for Wally once. It was his twelfth birthday if I'm remembering right. Everyone was invited. We were all standing around watching him blow out the candles when we heard a scream. A cousin of his had tumbled down the stairs. We rushed to help her, but when I looked up I saw Consuelo standing at the top landing, grinning like a cat who had just cleaned a saucer full of cream."

"What happened?"

"The cousin broke her arm and was taken to the hospital, but I later heard rumors she was paid not to make a stink."

"You said rumors."

"Ah, yeah. My girlfriends said Consuelo had pushed the poor girl down the stairs for making fun of her dress."

"Did anyone see Consuelo push the girl?"

"If they did, no one has ever said."

"Can you give me something that witnesses actually saw Consuelo do?"

"Not exactly. People like the Hoppers don't work out in the open, Mona. It's always your word against theirs when something happens."

"How old was Consuelo at this time?"

"I'd say about twenty-two. Things only got worse when Dexter Deatherage dumped her for Wilhelmina. She then became indiscreet with one of the servants and was finally shipped off to Venice with orders not to come back."

"Anything else?"

Melanie thought for a moment. "Did anyone tell you the story that Hedda Hopper, Connie's first wife, fell off a ladder trimming the Christmas tree and died?"

"Yes."

"Don't believe it. She was found hanging from the balustrade."

"Suicide?"

"Or murder. Everyone knew Hedda died from hanging, but the newspapers reported her death as an accident from falling off a ladder. That shows you right there that the Hoppers had clout and still do. Their name still means something in this town."

"What else about Mrs. Hopper's death?"

"There was no suicide note, and at that time, Connie was having financial difficulties. I know we don't see eye-to-eye, but you shouldn't mess with the Hopper family. Something's not right there. Wally, Connie, and Consuelo are all cut from the same cloth, except Consuelo is meaner, and she's back for a reason."

"Do you feel Elspeth is in danger?"

Melanie put a finger on her lips, pondering. "Let me see. Her maid has been stabbed in the back and there are no suspects. Um, what do you think? We all know that little stump of a black man didn't kill the maid." Melanie cackled. "How could he even reach up that far to stab her unless he had a chair? The Sheriff's just making a big show."

"Have you met Elspeth?"

"Yes."

"What did you think?"

"A babe in the woods compared to the Hoppers. She should watch her back."

"Anything else?"

"I'll have to go down memory lane, but I used to keep a diary at that age. I'll go through and call if I find anything else."

Mona stood. "Thank you, Melanie. Once these stories are confirmed, I'll deposit the money."

"I prefer cash, if you don't mind."

"As you wish."

"Show yourself out, Niece, and don't let the door hit you in the you-know-what on your way out."

Mona didn't hear Melanie's last words. She was distracted—thinking that she needed a clever, silver-tongue devil to root out the truth. There was only one man for this job.

Rupert Hunt!

21

Mona and Violet were packing for the upcoming weekend at the Netherland Plaza in Cincinnati when a knock sounded on the bedroom door.

"Come in," Violet said.

Dotty poked her head in the room. "Mona, Rupert is here. Samuel is watching in case Rupert decides to steal the silver."

Violet snickered.

"Show Rupert to the library, and Dotty, you better stay with him until I come down."

Dotty grinned. "Understood." She closed the door and hurried back to the mansion's foyer where Rupert was cooling his heels.

"Do you think Rupert found anything?" Violet asked, wrapping a pair of black velvet evening shoes for Mona's luggage.

"I'll know in a few moments." Mona looked askance at the dresses and coats strewn about her bed. "Look at this. When I first came here, I had just the clothes on my back and what I had purchased in Cincinnati. Now, I'm traveling with a steamer trunk for just two days. When did my life become so complicated?"

"Clothes are symbols. They state a person's power."

"So you do really believe clothes make the woman. Violet, I had no idea you were such a philosopher."

"You know those paintings of Queen Elizabeth I with her jewels, ruffles, and fancy gowns. She believed those clothes screamed her status and helped her to retain power."

Mona was astonished. "Goodness, Violet. When I first came here, you didn't even know who Elizabeth I was!"

"Did you know she was known as the Virgin Queen and wore pearls because they symbolized purity?"

"Really," Mona replied, amused.

"And it is thought those same pearls make up

the current pearls sewn on the English crown." Violet closed her eyes. "Isn't the Prince of Wales just dreamy? He's so handsome. Any girl would be lucky to catch him."

"Hmm," Mona murmured, wondering if the rumors were true that the Prince of Wales, commonly known as David, was sympathetic to Adolph Hitler. Giving Violet a gentle squeeze, Mona asked, "Finish for me, will you? I'm going downstairs to see what Rupert wants."

"Sure. What shall I pack?"

"Whatever you want. I'll leave it to you."

"Good, then I'm throwing your black velvet gown out of the running. You wear it too much. You've got to look smart on this trip. You're representing the House of Moon."

"Lock the door after me," Mona said. "Remember, Rupert's in the house."

Violet grinned, but shuddered after Mona closed the door. She'd be glad when Rupert Hunt was gone.

Mona hurried to the library where she found Rupert drinking her good port and smoking a cigar while Samuel stood in the corner, glaring at him.

"Hello, Rupert."

Rupert jumped to his feet and bowed. "Greetings, Mona, misty maiden of the Moon millions."

"How was your trip from Montana?" Mona said, sitting opposite Rupert before the fire. She waved for Samuel to leave.

"Uneventful until I arrived here. I was strip-searched and thoroughly humiliated by those Pinkerton gorillas at your beck and call. What's the matter, Mona? Lose your trust in your fellow man?"

"I wouldn't have had the need for those gorillas if it hadn't been for you."

"Ah, not true. They were around when I first came to tea on that fateful Tuesday."

Mona knitted her brows together. "Let's not talk about that, shall we?"

"You had to admit it was clever of me."

"Your clever plan got poor Chester Combs killed."

Agitated, Rupert shook his head. "That was never part of my plan. Nobody was to be hurt. Blame it on that nurse, Althea."

"Let's not go into it. You were to gather information for me."

Rupert pulled a report from his pocket. "I read all the Pinkerton reports along with Deatherage's notes."

"You were to get info from your contacts in Europe."

Rupert nodded, handing the report to Mona. "I did."

Mona looked sideways at the report, "This is awfully slim."

Rupert tapped the report with his index finger. "But the details are dynamite."

"Suppose you tell me."

"First, let's start with Grandma Hopper. I was able to track down her admission form into Eastern State Hospital. It took some doing as she was registered under her maiden name."

"What was the cause?"

"There's a copy in the report, but it basically said she was suffering from 'female hysteria' and prone to violent outbreaks. Grandma was in the bunny hatch for three months and then released. After that, there is no record of her until she dies in 1919."

"Female hysteria means the doctors didn't know what was wrong. Could also mean hubby didn't like her carping at him. Men used the threat of the insane asylum to control women."

"Wasn't there a Sherlock Holmes story about that?"

"You're thinking of *The Adventures of the Copper Beeches.* An heiress was sequestered because of her fortune."

"Oh."

"Let's get back to the subject at hand. What about the admitting doctor?"

"He's dead and his files have been destroyed. I checked."

"Any other psychiatric treatment for a Hopper family member?"

Rupert shrugged. "None that I could find and besides researching state institutions, where would I look?"

"I see. What about Hedda Hopper's death?"

"Well, the death certificate is in the file. She died from an accidental cervical fracture."

"A cervical fracture is a broken neck. Wouldn't that cause immediate death? I heard she lived several days after."

"I guess it depends on how serious the damage to the spinal cord. I'm no doctor.

However, I tracked down some old servants and I found one Anna Mae Winfred, who worked at the Hopper house as a young girl. She said she was told by one of the farm laborers that he cut a noose from an upstairs balustrade and was told to burn the rope and keep quiet about it."

"Can we find this laborer?"

"Dead." Rupert noticed Mona raised a questioning eyebrow. "Natural causes. I checked."

"Any other police reports?"

"Nothing besides Cornelius' father passing bad checks back in the day."

"What about Cadwallader Hopper?"

"Nothing criminal about him. He is personally disliked by his colleagues and considered ruthless in his business dealings, but nothing illegal that I could find. Wally Hopper is just a pain in the fanny. Nothing to hang your hat on there."

"Consuelo?"

Rupert leaned forward. "Now, she's a piece of work. Consuelo is a well-known socialite in Italy with her home base in Venice. She was shipped overseas before the Great War and became the mistress of several important politically-connected men—all with fascist leanings."

"Consuelo stayed in Italy during the war?"

"Yes, she did. Like I said the old gal has connections. Apparently, Consuelo is witty, bright, and sexually adventurous, but her charms are fading as they say, and she has been cut loose by her latest amour."

"Is she broke?"

"On the contrary, she owns a home on the Grand Canal and a beach hut in Bermuda. She always wears the latest fashions and collects avant-garde art such as Picasso, Miro, Matisse, you know, artists like that."

Mona was trying to place the artists. She had heard of Picasso and Matisse, but was not familiar with Miro's work or any of the other avant-garde artists.

"Here's the kicker. I traced this Beulah Bradley, and she lived in Venice for a year in 1928."

"Really! Now that is interesting. Was she a servant?"

Rupert grinned. "She was a socialite and palled around with all the swells on equal footing."

"That's interesting. What's Beulah's backstory?"

"She rented a palazzo on a side canal in the less desirable part of Venice, but was invited to all the grand parties and social events. She was known as the daughter of John Alden."

"Did Beulah go by the last name of Alden?"

"Bradley, but you must remember the Italians are not so fussy about parentage as the British are."

"Or the Americans." Mona was lost in thought for a moment. "It would seem likely that Beulah and Consuelo knew each other, then."

"Don't it, though. That's all I've got at the moment."

Mona rose and went over to her desk to retrieve an envelope. "Here's a bonus, but keep digging. Find out all that you can."

Rupert looked in the envelope and thumbed the crisp twenty-dollar bills. "If I had known that working for you on the up-and-up would have been so lucrative, I never would have kidnapped you."

Mona frowned. "The less you say about that event, the better, Rupert."

"Yes, Boss. I'll see myself out, Boss."

Mona rang the servant's cord. "Samuel will

see you out of the house, and the Pinkertons will see you off the property."

Rupert feigned hurt. "You act like you don't trust me."

"Goodbye, Rupert."

"Goodbye, Boss." Rupert waved the envelope at Mona. "Until we meet again."

Samuel entered the room and escorted a jubilant Rupert Hunt out of the library.

"Not if I can help it, Rupert," Mona said under her breath. "Not if I can help it."

22

Mona finished packing, leaving the suitcases by her bedroom door, ready to be carried down to the car. She, Lord Farley, and the Deatherages planned to catch the night train to Cincinnati. They would be at the Netherland Plaza in time for a late supper and dancing until the wee hours of the morning.

The phone rang once and fell silent. Mona assumed it had been answered by Thomas downstairs. A few minutes later, Violet poked her head in the door. "Miss Mona, Lord Farley is on the phone."

"Thank you, Violet."

Mona picked up the phone. "Robert, I'm ready. Are you going to pick me up?"

"Darling, I'm afraid my plans have changed

for the weekend."

"Oh, Robert, don't."

"I just got a call that my father has had a heart attack. I'll join you on the train to Cincinnati. After that, I'll catch the red-eye to New York and then a ship to Plymouth."

"Robert, is your father very ill?"

"Father's doctor wouldn't have called if he wasn't. It sounds serious."

"I'll ride with you to Cincinnati and then catch the return train home in the morning."

"Go on with the Deatherages and have fun this weekend. Go see Will Rogers like we planned."

"How can I? No. No. I'll accompany you to Cincinnati to see you off and then come home. I can't have any fun without you."

"It would be wonderful if you could. I feel bad about ruining your weekend."

"Don't give it a second thought. This is much more important."

"You don't mind? I am so sorry about this."

"It can't be helped, Robert."

"I might be gone a long time, Mona."

"I hadn't thought of that," Mona said, realizing Robert might never come back if his father died. "Don't worry about any of that now. We've got a train to catch. I'll send the car around for you. Are you ready?"

"Ready as I'll ever be."

"See you in a moment," Mona said. "And Robert."

"Yes?"

"Everything will be all right."

But Mona didn't believe a word of what she said.

23

Mona looked at her social calendar, noting that Robert had been gone for almost a month. She hadn't heard from Robert during the last week. It was not like him not to write at least once a day.

Anxious and bored for something to do, Mona and Chloe hitched a ride with one of her workers to the feed store in Versailles. Snow still blanketed the Bluegrass, and most people stayed tucked in their warm homes. However, Mooncrest Farm's horses needed grain, and Mona was experiencing cabin fever. She needed to get out even if it meant sharing a bouncy, smelly truck with a talkative, cigar-chewing driver. Reaching the grain store, Mona hopped down and went into the store, breathing in the scents of molasses, cracked corn, hay bales, leather, and smoke from a potbellied stove. She sat in one of the chairs before the stove, closed her eyes, and rocked as she waited for her employee to finish loading the truck. It was good to be out of the house.

"Hello there, Miss Moon."

Mona looked up and spied Sheriff Gideon standing over her sporting his big Stetson hat. "Hello, Sheriff."

"I'm surprised to see you here without your bodyguards."

Mona put a finger to her lips. "Shh. They don't know I snuck out."

"May I?" Gideon said, pointing to a rocking chair. He petted Chloe, who was sniffing his pant legs and shoes.

"Please do. It's quite comfy rocking before the stove."

"What brings you to my part of the world?"

Mona thumbed to her truck. "My horses need grain."

"Glad I ran into you."

"How is your wife, Sheriff?"

"Middlin'"

"I'm sorry."

"She was right tickled about the cake you sent home with me. It helped put some weight on her."

"Good. Good."

"I hear you have problems of your own, though."

"What would that be?"

"I hear tell that Lord Farley went back to England."

"His father is very ill."

"Kinda' puts you in a bind."

"Doesn't put me in a bind at all, Sheriff."

Sheriff Gideon studied Mona. "Jellybean Martin got bailed out and is walking around free as a bird."

"Heard that."

"You wouldn't have anything to do with paying his bail, would you, Miss Moon?"

Mona smiled and rocked.

Sheriff Gideon fell into the rhythm of rocking with her. "It doesn't matter. I was going to drop the charges against him anyway."

Mona stopped rocking. "Why is that?"

"Jellybean doesn't have a motive plus there is

no evidence to show he committed the murder."

Mona looked sideways at the Sheriff, who wore a self-satisfied smirk. "I guess you made that up about Jellybean's fingerprints being on the knife."

"You're not the only who can be evasive, Miss Moon. I knew he was your man. I just wanted to shake the tree and see what fell out."

"So whose fingerprints were on the knife?"

"It doesn't matter about the knife."

Mona was perplexed. "Why not?"

"Because Beulah Bradley died from being hit in the head by a rock. She basically bled to death!"

24

"Trauma to the head! Didn't see that coming." Mona resumed rocking and was silent for a few minutes. She realized she was sitting next to a master of the ruse. Sheriff Gideon was a trickster. It sounded a contradiction for a member of law enforcement to lie in order to find out the truth. Unfortunately, sometimes one had to leave a trail of cracked corn to see which chickens took the bait. Mona could see Sheriff Gideon and Rupert Hunt were cut from the same cloth. They just worked different sides of the street. "Why are you telling me this? I thought private citizens were not privy to details of a criminal investigation."

"I know you had another man snooping around, and I want to know what he found out. I don't have the resources you have."

"Are you asking me for my help, Sheriff?"

"Yes, ma'am, I am. I know you think I've been hard, but I'm just trying to get at the facts. I want any information your man has."

"What do I get in return?"

"I can get a warrant for the information, Miss Moon. Don't try my patience."

"Oh, Sheriff, play along. Give me the details of the case, and I'll give you those files. Today, if you like."

"Quid pro quo, again?"

"Precisely."

"What do you want to know?"

"How do you know it wasn't arsenic poisoning or did you make that up, too?"

"Oh, no, Miss Bradley was sick with the stuff. I imagined she realized someone was poisoning her. That's why she fixed her own meals and ate by herself."

"Did you find out how she was poisoned?"

"Sugar bowl—her personal sugar bowl. Seems she had a sweet tooth and liked sugar in her tea."

"Loose sugar or cubed?"

"Cubed."

"Is your theory the poisoner was irritated that

Beulah hadn't kicked the bucket yet, and took a more direct action?"

"Leaning in that direction."

"Did you know that Beulah Bradley was John Alden's eldest daughter?"

Sheriff Gideon took out a bandanna handkerchief and wiped his neck. "Don't that beat all. Brings up some interesting notions in my head." He moved his rocking chair back from the stove, as it was getting too hot.

Mona did likewise.

"What else do you know?"

"It's not what I know, Sheriff. It's what the Hopper family knew. Did they know about Beulah being Elspeth's half-sister, and is there a reason they wanted that kept quiet?"

"You're going in the wrong direction with this."

"Okay, Sheriff, which direction are you going?"

"One—I already had guessed that Beulah and Elspeth were somehow related. I had discovered the picture of Miss Bradley with John Alden, which your maid, Violet, stole. That's evidence, Miss Moon. I'd like to have the picture back."

Mona grinned. "It will be with my man's file."

"Two—If your maid had searched more thoroughly, she would have found a loose floorboard under the bed. My men found it two days earlier and discovered a large wad of bills. Now the interesting thing was some of the bills are Italian."

"Liras."

"Exactly."

"She lived in Venice years ago."

"These bills were fresh."

"That brings Consuelo Hopper into the fold, then. She has just come from Venice recently."

"So I'm told."

"You think Consuelo Hopper killed Beulah?"

"Too early to tell yet, but I'm piecing the puzzle together."

"What other goodies do you have to tell me?"

"Three—I'm leaning on the motive of blackmail."

"I had thought of that."

"Think on it some more." Sheriff Gideon stood. "Nice talking with you, Miss Moon. I'll have a man pick up that file later this afternoon." He tipped the brim of his hat and strode out of the feed store.

Still waiting on her employee, Mona got out of the rocking chair and wandered about the store. Finding a display of flower seed packets, she picked an array of various flower packets to take back with her. After all, spring was right around the corner—or so the locals said.

After paying for the seeds, she selected a few more packets, and after paying for them, asked the clerk, "Can you deliver these to Sheriff Gideon's wife, please? They might give her some pleasure."

The clerk looked puzzled. "Did you say Sheriff Gideon's wife?"

"Yes. Can you deliver these seeds to her?"

The clerk scratched his chin. "Well, ma'am, I would, but Sheriff Gideon doesn't have a wife. He's a bachelor man."

Mona swirled around, looking to see if Sheriff Gideon was still in the parking lot. She wanted a word with him. "That dirty dog!" was all she could mutter.

25

Several weeks had gone by and no arrests had been made in the murder of Beulah Bradley. Charges were dropped against Jellybean Martin, and he caught the train back to Detroit feeling that Lexington was still too hot for him.

Each morning, Mona read the paper to see if an arrest had been made, but nothing was written about the case. Occasionally, Mona would lay the contents of Beulah's file out on her desk and study the reports, but nothing jumped out at her. She knew the solution to the case was right in front of her. The answer had to be in those reports somewhere, but where?

The days seemed to drag on without Robert. He called every Sunday, but sounded over-wrought, and although his letters were cheerful,

Mona sensed something foreboding about them. She wondered if Robert had started drinking again. Mona pushed those thoughts behind her, believing she had to trust him. Though she kept busy with business meetings and social activities, Mona missed Robert terribly. She realized she had fallen deeply in love with Robert and worried that their relationship might not work out. Robert promised he would be back by early spring, but his father's health was still precarious. Mona wasn't sure if he could keep that promise. She had to keep busy and enjoy life as best she could without him. The one event Mona was looking forward to was Violet receiving her high school diploma.

Wearing her new dress with the white piping, Violet had a party at her mother's home after she had passed her high school equivalence test. Her tutor presented Violet with her diploma while Mona and Dotty watched. Mona swelled with pride as she knew how hard Violet had worked to finish high school.

"Speech! Speech," Dotty called out.

Violet looked at her mother and friends with tears in her eyes. "This Depression has kicked the floor out for many of us. None of us realized the grief it would cause our families and our communities, but I have found that if we work together and give each other a helping hand, we can get through this tempest. I was resigned to quitting school and being a maid all my life, which can be a rewarding life. Finishing high school was not important to me, but Miss Mona made me see that education for a woman is a must. It gives a woman choices in life. We don't have to be dependant upon anyone because we can develop skills, get a job, and make our own way in life. Now if I wish to stay a lady's maid, I can, but if I want to try my hand at something else, I have the ability to do so." She held up her diploma. "Miss Mona, this diploma is as much yours as it is mine. Thank you."

Mona gave a little bow and held up her glass of punch. "Here's to you, Violet!"

Dotty gave Mona a little nudge and whispered. "Violet seems to have a flair for the dramatic. Tempest? That's a big word for a maid."

Ignoring Dotty's dig, Mona helped herself to a piece of chocolate cake with marshmallow icing made by Violet's mother.

Noticing Mona's sour face, Dotty said, "I'm sorry, Mona. I stepped out of line."

"Violet is a fledgling flapping her wings. Let's encourage her to fly, shall we? Sisterhood and all that."

"Mona, I really didn't mean anything with that crack."

"I know you didn't, Dotty, but words matter."

"Words are just words, Mona."

"No, words are worlds."

"You're talking over my head."

Mona had realized something important about Dotty. She was an efficient secretary—expedient, cheerful, and fun, but some issues were beyond her grasp.

Mona handed Dotty some cake. "Let's forget it. Have some cake."

"I'd love to, but I've got to run to town."

"It's late. What for?"

"I'm picking up my typewriter. I had it cleaned and the letter E replaced. It looked more like a G than an E. You know, Mr. Deatherage should get his typewriter cleaned, too. All his correspondence has the lower case i with no dot.

Drives me crazy." Dotty looked at her watch. "If I want to get your letters typed for tomorrow's post, I need to dash now. Save me a piece of cake, will ya?"

Mona nodded and watched Dotty leave in one of the farm's cars. Something in their conversation had struck a chord, but Mona couldn't quite place her finger on it. Sitting near the living room coal stove, Mona ate her cake, thinking about the phrase—words are worlds. Suddenly, everything fell into place about the death of Beulah Bradley. Well, most things. Mona needed to get a hold of Sheriff Gideon fast or else another murder might take place.

26

Mona was escorted into the drawing room. She sat with her coat on as no fire was lit in the fireplace, and the room was chilly. Like mansions in England, the Hopper home had no central heat.

Fifteen minutes later, Connie strode in. He was wearing work pants and muddy boots, Mona knew that he had been fetched from the barns, and he was tracking filth on the Persian carpets. Mona thought back to the need for two front doors of Keene Place. "Miss Mona, so nice to see you again, but did you have an appointment with Elspeth? She's feeling a bit under the weather today, and I don't think she's up to seeing anyone. Is there something I can do for you?"

"That's just it. I've been calling for over a

week, and Elspeth has not gotten back to me. Naturally, I came to check on her."

Connie looked perplexed. "I don't know why she hasn't returned your calls, but she hasn't been feeling well the last several weeks. That's probably why."

Alarmed, Mona stood up. "Hasn't been feeling well?"

"No, she's been complaining of stomach cramps."

"Mr. Hopper."

"Connie, please."

"Okay, Connie. You need to see your wife immediately and check her fingernails. If there are white horizontal lines on her nails, she must get to a hospital and be tested for heavy metal poisoning."

Connie almost fell backwards from shock and glanced at the ceiling. "Surely, you don't mean arsenic?"

"I do, sir."

"I'll go up at once."

"I'm going home. Will you please ring me regardless of the outcome?"

"Yes, of course. Please see yourself out."

Connie rushed out of the room while Mona followed him into the foyer. She watched him go up the grand staircase, presumably to check on his wife.

Mona would know soon enough about Elspeth as she had Pinkertons watching the mansion. The only thing she could do now was go home and wait for Connie's call—if he called.

27

Mona had just taken off her hat and given her coat to Samuel when he told her that she had received a telegram. It was on her desk in the library. She thanked him and asked for a sandwich and some tea. Chloe jumped up only to have Mona push her away. "Not now, Chloe. Give me a minute." Mona hurried to the library where she found the telegram and opened it.

MONA. STOP. FATHER WORSE THAN EXPECTED. STOP. DON'T KNOW WHEN I'LL BE BACK. STOP. THINK ABOUT COMING TO ENGLAND. STOP. ALL MY LOVE ROBERT. STOP

Dismayed, Mona sank in her chair with Chloe nudging her hand. The telegram worried Mona. If Robert didn't telephone this Sunday, she was going to call him. Apparently, things were not going well in England or else Robert would write to her more often. He must be very distracted with something. Mona decided to write to Lady Alice and have her check on Robert as well. Mona needed to know what was going on with her betrothed.

A knock sounded on the door. "Come in."

Samuel brought in a tray of sandwiches and a pot of hot tea.

"Thank you for lighting the fire."

"I know you like a toasty room, but then no one likes the cold, do they?"

"I don't. Been cold too often in my life."

"Monsieur Bisaillon made the egg salad for the sandwiches fresh this morning and there are cucumber and cream cheese sandwiches too. He cut the crust just way you like them."

"Where in the world did he get a fresh cucumber?"

"In our new hothouse."

"Oh, yes. I forgot about that. Tell Monsieur Bisaillon I thank him."

"He says he has a nice dinner waiting for you—some poached salmon and roasted potatoes and a nice lemon tart for dessert."

"Sandwiches are fine this evening. Have the kitchen staff and Monsieur Bisaillon enjoy the salmon and the lemon tarts."

Samuel looked at Mona's glum face. "Bad news, Miss Mona?" He poured tea into a cup and handed it to her.

"Not really, but not great either."

Mona gave a faint smile, knowing her staff was waiting in the kitchen for news about the telegram. Telegrams were always harbingers of bad news. "Tell everyone that they are not going to lose their jobs. Nothing has happened with Mooncrest Enterprises. Everything is fine and dandy. This was a personal telegram."

Samuel sighed with relief. "Lord Farley doing fine, then?"

Mona chuckled. "You are the worst gossip, Samuel. Why ask me when you can listen through the heat ducts?"

Samuel grinned. "You rerouted the heating system. Can't use those ducts like we did before. I have to get my information from other means."

"I assure you nothing is wrong. You may leave."

"Shall I take Chloe with me?"

"Leave her. I'm sure she will enjoy the egg salad sandwiches as much as I will."

"I won't be telling our chef that you will be sharing his sandwiches with Chloe."

Mona tilted her head. "Good thinking. Where's Violet?"

"Up in your suite. Shall I send for her?"

"No, I'll be up in an hour or so. I won't be needing you again tonight."

"Good night, Miss Mona."

"Good night, Samuel."

Mona waited until Samuel closed the library door before she threw the telegram into the fire. She put her head into her hands. What to do? What to do?

28

Mona didn't get a call from Connie Hopper until late the next day. The doctors said Elspeth was indeed suffering from arsenic poisoning. Mona replied she was very sorry but not surprised.

Connie thanked Mona for alerting him. "I just didn't put two and two together. I've tried to put Beulah's death behind us, so I wasn't making the connection. Who could be doing these awful things? I don't know what to think."

"I understand your frustration. Was Sheriff Gideon notified?"

"I don't know. Maybe the hospital called him, but I haven't seen him around."

"Be careful what you eat, Connie. Have you had yourself tested?"

"Why no. I never thought of it."

"It would be wise that everyone at your home be tested, including the servants."

"Even the servants? Oh, this is just horrible."

"Yes, the servants as well as your family," Mona insisted. "You don't know the source of the arsenic. Until you find the source, it is better to be safe."

There was silence on the phone for a moment until Connie said, "You're quite right. I'll make arrangements. Thank you, again, Mona."

Mona heard the phone click. She sat and thought for a moment while scratching Chloe's ears. "Chloe, I think it's time I do something about this Hopper matter before someone else gets hurt or worse."

Chloe barked as if in agreement.

"And it is time to do something about Lord Farley. Don't you agree, pretty girl?"

Chloe barked again and wagged her tail.

Mona could have sworn the dog was smiling.

29

Mona found the hospital room, lightly knocked on the door, and poked her head inside. "Elspeth, are you decent?"

"Come in, Mona. Come in. So nice to see someone."

"Wow, look at all the flowers. Who sent them?"

"Mostly friends of Connie's wishing me good health, but even Wally and Consuelo sent arrangements. It's very lovely to have color in this drab room." Elspeth looked admiringly at Mona's black and beige suit with a triangle hat sporting a peacock feather in its band. "You look awfully smart, Mona."

Mona swirled around. "You like? My maid stitched this up for me. I told you she was clever with a needle and thread."

"She did a good job mending my clothes. I never thanked her properly. I was very distracted with Beulah's death. What was her name again?"

"Violet. Her name is Violet."

"I do remember Dotty's name. She was most helpful. Thanking Violet will be on my list of things to do when I get out of this place. Oh, you wouldn't believe how horrible the food is. It's a sordid mess."

Mona pulled a chair up to Elspeth's bed and took off her gloves. "Yes, I do believe it. I had lunch in the cafeteria before coming to your room. Just something quick, you see. I'm afraid my broccoli was cooked to death, although they do have a large selection of Jell-O salads."

"Dreadful stuff."

"I concur except for cherry. I like cherry Jell-O with banana slices."

There was a pause between the two women until Elspeth said, "Thank you for coming, Mona. I'm a little tired right now, so if you don't mind, I'd like to take a nap.

"I do mind."

"What did you say?"

"It's time you come clean, Elspeth."

"Whatever do you mean?"

"You poisoned yourself."

Elspeth shot up in bed. "I did what!"

"It was clever of you to risk your life ingesting the same poison you fed to Beulah, but you had to throw suspicion on someone else. Will the police find a bottle of rat poison in Wally's room? My money is on you framing Consuelo."

"If they do, it only proves Consuelo murdered Beulah."

Mona shook her head. "I'm afraid not. Beulah was being poisoned long before Consuelo returned to Kentucky. The timeline is wrong."

"How would you know?"

"Beulah prepared her own food and ate in her room since she came to the Bluegrass. She had grown suspicious she was being poisoned. That was before either Wally or Consuelo showed up. Did Beulah confront you on the night of the reception? Is that why you were crying in your room? You knew you had been caught and were worried what Beulah might do. I don't think Connie said anything at all about your dress. It was all just a ploy to get my sympathy."

"How dare you suggest that I would poison Beulah? I don't know what you are talking about. Get out! Get out, I say!"

"Not before we have a serious talk. I think you were going to kill Beulah the night of your reception. She confronted you and left your suite to lock herself in her room. Why else would a maid not be present to help her mistress on the night of a huge reception? You were thinking of how to kill her once and for all during the ball, and you heard me ask the downstairs maid if I could use the upstairs powder room. I might prove to be a useful alibi for you. You left your door open ever so slightly knowing I would hear you crying."

Elspeth spat out. "I'm going to call the nurse and have you thrown out."

"But things took a turn when I insisted you change your dress and go back downstairs. I wasn't easy to manipulate and you couldn't get rid of me fast, so you had to put your plan to kill Beulah on hold for that night, at least."

"I won't dignify your accusations. I thought you were my friend."

"Let's talk about the letters first. I always

wondered why you came to me about them until I realized you were throwing mud at the wall and seeing what stuck. You were desperate to find a scapegoat, which was to be me until Consuelo came home."

Elspeth closed her eyes and looked away. "You are a demon. Yes, a demon in the form of a woman."

"You wrote those threatening letters. That's why they were made of letters cut from magazines. Number one—you couldn't write them because your handwriting would be analyzed. Everyone's handwriting is discernible, even their printing. Number two—you couldn't use a typewriter as the typing could be traced back to a particular typewriter, so you had to use cutout letters."

"Why would I do such a thing?"

"Again, to throw mud on the wall to see what stuck because you had decided in England to murder Beulah. That's when you started poisoning her. Once the Aldrich-Mees lines started exhibiting on her fingers, Beulah realized why she was feeling ill."

"How would you know Beulah was feeling ill in England?"

"I'm guessing, but it will be easy to verify. All Sheriff Gideon would have to do is check with your staff in England and ask them."

"So what if Beulah had upset stomachs in England? Means she ate something which didn't agree with her."

"Let's talk about the envelopes. I always wondered why you said you threw away the envelopes. That didn't make sense to me. You were academically trained. You know every bit of evidence is important, having learned from your father who was known for notating details. It was because there were no envelopes. Never were. In fact, I think no one knew of these letters until you showed them to me. You did a great job of making the paper look worn and tired."

"You fascinate me, Mona. Go on with your fairytale."

"The problem was that Beulah wouldn't die. Once she confronted you about the poisoning, you couldn't sneak the rat arsenic into her food like you had before, so you put it in her sugar bowl which was locked in her room."

"So how could I poison her then if her room was locked?"

"I went to your house before coming here and found a spare key on top of the door jamb of your room."

"The key to my room."

"That key unlocked Beulah's door."

"Anybody could have switched keys and put Beulah's key on top of my door jamb. Wally and Consuelo hate me. They probably put Beulah's key there."

Mona continued, "Then there was the over-kill. Beulah was poisoned, hit with a rock, and stabbed in the back. Only someone who hated Beulah would go to such links. What was the problem? Wouldn't she die? You stabbed her and she still lived, so you hit her in the head with a rock."

Elspeth muttered something under her breath.

"What was that? I didn't catch it."

"If anyone hated Beulah, it was Consuelo. They met each other in Venice when Beulah lived there a short time."

"I heard they were friends and ran around in the same circles."

"They ran around in the same circles, but they were not friends."

"Clue me in."

"Beulah was blackmailing Consuelo because she knew her secret."

Mona was taken back for a moment. "What secret?"

"You think you know everything. Here's a corker for you. Wally is not Connie's son. He's Consuelo's out-of-wedlock bastard. He and his first wife took Wally as their own son to protect the family secret. They went on an extended tour of Europe and came back with Wally."

Mona was momentarily caught off guard. "Did Consuelo know that Beulah was your sister?"

Now, Elspeth looked stunned. "What are you talking about?"

"Sheriff Gideon found a picture of your father with a girl who looked very similar to Beulah."

"How would you know? You never saw Beulah in person."

"Is that why Beulah's casket was closed, so as not to expose how similar Beulah's features were to yours? There's no way you could not have known Beulah was your half-sister, and it would explain why no one outside the family ever saw

Beulah. The servants said she was your constant companion, but you always left her in the car or hidden away when guests came to your home."

"Consuelo is the real killer—not me. She comes home after being an expat for nearly two decades and discovers the woman who has been bleeding her dry all those years is living in her ancestral home. It must have been a shock. She couldn't afford Beulah exposing her secret after all this time, so she conspired to meet Beulah alone in the middle of the night and killed her."

"Again, the timeline doesn't match up. Also, Consuelo knew Beulah was John Alden's daughter years ago. If she wanted to kill her, why not in Venice, where she could have killed her years earlier? Here's what I think happened. You met Connie Hopper at a party in London and put two and two together. You knew of Beulah's association with Connie's sister, Consuelo, and hatched your plan to marry him because you were wanting to shed Beulah once and for all."

"But you haven't given a motive yet. Without a motive, this is all conjecture. Consuelo is the person with a motive."

"You're right. It is circumstantial at best. I

can't prove any of this, but it must have been a shock when you discovered Beulah had been secretly selling your father's fabled artifacts and replacing them with fakes."

"I don't know what you are talking about," Elspeth said, swallowing hard.

"As I said, both Sheriff Gideon and I went to your house before coming here."

"Why you?"

"Because I know something about antiquities. You forget my background."

"You know nothing about Egyptian art or jewelry."

"I know enough to recognize a fake when I see it."

Elspeth hissed, "Ya Gazma."

Mona raised an eyebrow at the insult. "The gold in your wesekh is not authentic to the period. It overlays silver."

"Means nothing. No one can wear one hundred percent gold. It is too soft and will bend easily."

"I'm aware of that, Elspeth, but ancient Egyptians mixed other metals with their gold. They didn't put a layer of gold on top of pure silver."

"Ancient Egyptians used an alloy known as electrum which is gold, silver, and copper. Electrum was used to make Queen Ahsetsedek's jewelry."

Mona said, "They didn't layer gold over silver as silver was considered more precious than gold and a more valuable commodity. The original jeweler would have left the collar silver without the gold overlay, but Beulah didn't know that when she had the necklace counterfeited. She was not a trained academician."

"That collar is my property. You had no business examining it."

"Sheriff Gideon had a warrant. I merely scratched the back and discovered the silver. He has already sent the collar to the University of Kentucky and their antiquities department for analysis, but I think the Cincinnati Art Museum has already told you the news. They would have had to appraise the collection for the insurance. That's how you learned about the fakes."

"The plan for an exhibit is only recent. You accused me of poisoning Beulah in London."

"Sheriff Gideon took the liberty of calling the Cincinnati Art Museum and was told that the planning for the exhibit had been ongoing since early last year. He was also told you were notified that the proposal for the exhibit had been cancelled. You've known for a long time about the counterfeits. I'm sure not all pieces are fake, but maybe some of the most important ones such as Queens Ashsetsedek's collar.

Giving out a cry of despair, Elspeth ranted, "That horrible, horrible woman. Although my father never said, I knew the moment I saw Beulah who she was. We looked so much alike. My mother realized it, too, and hated having her in the house. It wasn't enough that my mother was ill, but he forced his illegitimate daughter upon us. From the beginning, Beulah took liberties with our possessions. I complained to Father, but he thought I was jealous and making up stories. Then I grew to realize that Beulah was putting Mother's life in danger, leaving her window open on cold nights and neglecting to give Mother her medicine. Still, Father wouldn't listen. Then Mother died and soon after, Father did also. I thought now I could get rid of this harridan, but when Beulah found out that Father had left everything to me, she flew into a rage.

Beulah threatened she would expose Father's secret of having an out-of-wedlock child and ruin his reputation further."

"Lots of men have trysts. Why would you care?"

"There was more. She found letters of Father's conspiring with British officials to smuggle artifacts out of Eypgt for money. I couldn't let my father's legacy be destroyed by those letters, so Beulah posed as my companion while she was sucking me dry. I'm glad she's dead. So very glad. I rejoiced the day we buried her. Fate was against me the day that woman came into my life."

"The fault, dear Brutus, lies not in our stars, but in ourselves."

"You know what you can do with your Shakespeare."

"Elspeth, you have provided a motive."

"I didn't confess to murdering Beulah. There is no evidence connecting me to Beulah's death. It's all circumstantial. Any good defense lawyer can make a case of Consuelo or even Wally killing Beulah. I'll get out of this, and when I do, I'll come looking for you."

Mona burst out laughing. "Tougher hombres

than you have tried to take me on, Elspeth, and they all failed." She picked up her purse. "See ya around, kid."

Elspeth let loose a number of vile Arabic curses as Mona left the room.

Sheriff Gideon stood in the hallway, waiting for Mona. They walked out of the hospital together.

"What was Mrs. Hopper yelling when you walked out of her room?"

"You don't want to know," Mona replied, wanly smiling.

"Hmm."

"I'm sorry, Sheriff Gideon. I couldn't break her."

"Mrs. Hopper is a tough cookie. I thought you could rattle her cage, and she would confess to murder. All she did was confess that she hated the woman." He opened the ward door for Mona. "It was a good try though, Miss Moon. A very good try. I couldn't have done better myself."

"Do you think the District Attorney will charge her with murder?"

Sheriff Gideon said, "I don't know. Even if

the artifacts are fakes, there is still the angle of Consuelo wanting to keep her secret about Wally under wraps. That could serve as a legitimate motive. I don't have any real physical evidence except for the key, but Mrs. Hopper is right. Anyone could have put the arsenic into Miss Bradley's sugar and then plant the key above Mrs. Hopper's door frame."

"Do you think Elspeth was telling the truth about Consuelo and Wally?"

"Unless I can find a birth certificate stating that Consuelo was Wally's biological mother, the only people who really know are Cornelius Hopper and his sister. I doubt Wally would have a clue about his real parentage, if what Elspeth says is true."

"You don't think Connie could be the father and Consuelo the mother?"

Sheriff Gideon's faced turned red. "That's indecent to even think such a thing much less say it out loud."

"It would explain a lot, though—maybe even as to the reason of the first Mrs. Hopper's death."

"Lordy, what a family. Consuelo is a sadist,

Wally is corrupt, the husband is passive-aggressive, his wife is a suspected murderess, and the wife's sister a blackmailer."

"Are you going to investigate Hedda Hopper's death?"

"I'm not going to open the case. It's very likely she did commit suicide by hanging herself, and the Hoppers covered it up. I checked out your information about that, and it rings true."

Mona accused, "You don't want to open it up."

"No, I don't because if I do, it will make my case against Elspeth Hopper weaker."

"I see." Mona motioned to Jamison to pull up the car. "I've done all I can for you, Sheriff. I wish you good luck."

"Thank you."

Mona got into the Daimler. "Oh, Sheriff. One more thing."

"Yes?"

"Give your wife my regards."

Sheriff Gideon grinned, tipped the brim of his Stetson, and winked. "I surely will."

30

Mona was perusing the morning paper's society column when she read Elspeth Hopper was going to Europe for a "cure." Everyone realized that meant a separation, and the Hopper marriage had failed. Mona threw down the paper in disgust. So it had been decided by the upper echelon in the Bluegrass that Sheriff Gideon would never arrest Elspeth Alden Hopper due to lack of evidence.

"What is it?"

"Nothing, Violet." Wanting to change the subject, Mona said, "It looks warmer today. Most of the snow has melted."

"I saw crocuses coming up in Mother's yard yesterday."

"Spring is quickly approaching," Mona said,

bending over to pet Chloe, lying next to her feet.

"Have you heard from Lord Farley?"

"He must be very busy," Mona said, not wishing to discuss Robert. She was terribly worried about him. Lady Alice had written that Robert was running himself ragged trying to save his family's estate from creditors. Apparently, the estate had been mismanaged for several years when his father had first taken ill.

"He used to write every day. Now you haven't heard from him in over two weeks."

"That's enough, Violet. Lord Farley is none of your concern."

Violet bit her lip. "I'm sorry."

"Nothing to be sorry about. Just don't bring him up anymore."

"I'm sure if Lord Farley was sick or injured, you would have received a telegram."

"VIOLET!"

Violet picked up her sewing basket and scurried away.

Mona took a deep breath. Violet was only voicing Mona's own concerns. Why hadn't she heard from Robert?

Mona motioned to the dog. "Let's go for a walk, Chloe."

The white poodle jumped up and pranced after Mona, who headed for the door.

Mona fetched her coat out of the closet and slipped out the front door, waving to the Pinkertons guarding Moon Mansion to stand down. "I'm going for a walk down the driveway. No need to follow. I have my gun with me."

"Okay, Boss," one of them said, knowing Mona was a crack shot. He went back to smoking a cigarette while the others huddled in their cars where it was warm.

Mona threw sticks for Chloe to fetch as she strolled down the driveway. The air was warmer and she could see bits of green in the lawn. Mindlessly, she kept playing with Chloe while wondering if something was wrong with Robert or had he met someone else. Out of the corner of her eye, she saw a black form jump the fence which divided Robert's and her property. Mona immediately stopped and pulled the gun from her pocket.

Frustrated that Mona was no longer throwing a stick, Chloe looked to where Mona was staring.

"You're a lousy watchdog, Chloe. You should have noticed that guy before I did."

Chloe barked gaily and ran toward the intruder.

"Chloe, come back!" Mona called.

The dog jumped into the arms of the figure. He hugged her and then put her down, as he made his way toward Mona.

Mona didn't know whether to run or shoot the intruder, but Chloe certainly knew him. Could it be? Mona stared at the figure coming toward her. The walk was so familiar. Yes, it had to be. It had to be!

Mona pocketed her gun and ran toward the approaching man, holding her arms outstretched. "ROBERT! ROBERT!

Lawrence Robert Emerton Dagobert Farley, Marquess of Gower, ran toward Mona calling her name.

They ran into each other's arms and embraced for the longest time with Robert kissing Mona's hair, her brow, her cheeks, and finally her lips.

Mona clung to him. "Why didn't you write?"

"Shut up, Mona. Just let me hold you. It's like I've been in the desert. I've got to drink you in." He buried his face in her neck. "Never again, Mona. Never again."

"No, darling. We will never be parted again. I've missed you so."

"I'm only half-a-man without you. You must promise me, Mona. No more of this shilly-shallying."

"You're right. We'll set a date for our wedding and never be apart again." Mona and Robert walked back to Moon Mansion arm-in-arm while Chloe joyously leapt on them. Sheriff Gideon, Elspeth Hopper, Jellybean Morton, and the other cast members of the Beulah Bradley murder faded from Mona's memory as she tucked it away to another part of her brain.

One day, Mona would take out that old file from her mind and dust it off, but right now she didn't care. Mona had a wedding to plan, and the Hoppers certainly wouldn't be invited.

Aldrich-Mees Lines

Two doctors who made the association of white lines perpendicular on a person's fingernails and arsenic poisoning.

Articles

Words that combine with a noun such as *the, a, and an* in the English language. However, Americans and the British use articles differently. An American would say, "I'm going to the hospital." An Englishman might say, "I am going to hospital."

Lord Farley often does not use articles in his sentences.

Arthur John Evans

In 1900, Sir Arthur Evans, an English archaeologist, began digging at Knossos on Crete and eventually discovered a grand palace and a forgotten ancient society. The palace suggested a labyrinth as in the King Minos legends which is why Evans named the newly discovered, bronze-aged civilization *Minoan* and distinguished it from a *Mycenaean Greek* civilization on the island. He also played a part in the formation of Yugoslavia.

Burgoo

A stew made with several different types of meat and vegetables for large gatherings.

French Campaign in Egypt

Napoleon Bonaparte invaded Egypt, then part of the Ottoman Empire, in 1798. Part of Bonaparte's goal was to weaken Great Britain's interest in the area and its access to India. During the campaign, Bonaparte ordered scientific studies of ancient Egypt and the Rosetta Stone was discovered, leading to the translation of ancient hieroglyphs by Jean-François Champollion for the first time in over two thousand years. After the French were defeated by the British, led by Horatio Nelson at the Battle of the Nile, the Rosetta Stone was transferred into British hands and now resides in the British Museum.

Cockney

A native of East London and with a distinct dialect associated with the working class.

Coptic Christians

One of the oldest sects of Egyptian Christians belonging to the Coptic Orthodox Church of

Alexandria, the largest Christian church in Egypt. Saint Mark is thought to be their founding father and is credited with writing the Gospel of Mark. Legend has it that the Venetians stole the body of Saint Mark, in 829 AD from Alexandria when rumors spread that the Muslims were going to destroy all Christian relics in the city. St. Mark rests in St. Mark's Cathedral in Venice—his symbol of the lion proudly displayed everywhere. The Coptic Orthodox Church in Alexandria also claims they have St. Mark's relics.

Ethan Frome
A 1911 novel by American author Edith Wharton, where the protagonist, Ethan Frome, and his lover, Mattie, are permanently injured while sledding down a hill.

Father Coughlin (1891-1979)
A Roman Catholic priest who became one of the first broadcasters to reach an audience of 30 million during the 1930s. His talks became almost as popular as President Roosevelt's fireside chats. As time progressed, Father Coughlin became a supporter of anti-Semitism and fascism, declaring admiration for Adolf Hitler and Mussolini. After

the outbreak of WWII, there were moves made by the US government to charge Coughlin with sedition, but Coughlin's superior, Bishop Mooney, fearing a backlash on the Catholic Church, ordered the priest to cease all political activities.

Five-and-Dime Store

Stores with a variety of items usually costing five or ten cents. Many had a snack area where customers sat on individual stools at a long bar facing the fry cook. They sold hamburgers, sandwiches, ice-cream, and soft drinks. For lunch, a *blue plate special* might be offered consisting of meatloaf, mashed potatoes, and peas. In Lexington, Ky, the five-and-dime was Woolworth's.

Heinrich Schliemann

A wealthy, amateur German archaeologist, obsessed with Homer's Iliad and Odyssey, began his search for the fabled city of Troy in 1871. Over the course of several years, he discovered a massive, ancient city which he proclaimed was Troy in Turkey and asserted that the legends were true. Unearthing priceless artifacts of gold, he smuggled *Priam's Treasure* from Turkey. The objects were displayed in the Pergamon Museum in Berlin until the artifacts, including jewelry, were stolen by the Russians in 1945. *Priam's Treasure* now resides in the Puskin Museum in Moscow. The Russians justified the theft due to the fact Russian museums had been looted by Germany when the Nazis invaded Russia in 1941.

Herbert Hoover

Thirty-first Republican president of the United States (1929-1933) and humanitarian. He is considered a failure as a president because he resisted federal intervention with relief efforts during the Great Depression. President Franklin D. Roosevelt won the 1932 election because of his New Deal platform which included federal work programs.

Howard Carter

A British archaeologist who discovered the intact tomb of an 18th Dynasty Pharaoh, Tutankhamun in 1922—considered one of the world's greatest archaeological finds. Despite this achievement, Carter received no honor from the British government. He died having never married.

John "Jack" Keene

John Keene sold his ancestral farm, which became Keeneland Race Course, one of the most beautiful racetracks in the USA. Besides being a premier racetrack, Keeneland is known for its good works such as distributing polio vaccinations to disadvantaged children during the 1950s. Keeneland Race Course in Lexington, Kentucky, opened on October 15, 1936 with 15,000 people attending opening day.

Lady Hester Stanhope

British adventurer who is considered the first archaeologist in the Holy Land for her expedition to Ashkelon in 1815. Her discovery of a medieval Italian manuscript led her to ask the Ottoman Empire for permission to dig which was granted. She is famous for the adage, "If someone asks you if you are a god, you say yes."

Margaret Mitchell

The author of *Gone With The Wind* secretly gave donations for African-American medical students to continue their education during a time of racial segregation and Ku Klux Klan public support. She reportedly put cash in a paper bag which was collected by someone in the African-American community and distributed.

Percy Shelley
Considered one of the major English Romantic poets of his age. His wife, Mary Shelley, wrote *Frankenstein*.

Prince of Wales
A title given to the heir apparent to the British throne. Edward Albert Christian George Andrew Patrick David Windsor was Prince of Wales in 1934. He became Edward VIII on January 20th, 1936, only to abdicate the same year because of his desire to marry Wallis Simpson, an American divorcee. It was unconstitutional for a ruler to marry a divorced person at that time.

Queen Ahsetsedek IV
Fabricated Egyptian queen for the purpose of this story.

Snogging
British slang for kissing.

Sultan Fuad
Ruler of Egypt, Nubia, Kordofan, and Darfur.

He was the ninth ruler of Egypt from the Muhammad Ali dynasty. Became king of Egypt in 1917 and substituted the title of King for Sultan when Egypt gained its independence from the British in 1922.

Valley of the Queens
Ninety known tombs of Egyptian queens and royal children.

Wesekh
Also referred to as an usekh. A type of broad collar worn by men and women in ancient Egypt by encircling the neck and supported by the neck and shoulders. Usually made of gold and semi-precious stones.

Whistlebritches
A Southern term for the sound corduroy makes when a person walks or a particularly fussy male.

Will Rogers (1879-1935)
Famous folksy entertainer and humorist born of a Cherokee family in the Cherokee Nation in Indian Territory, now known as Oklahoma. He would come out on stage and talk about current events while doing rope tricks with his lasso. He

made 70 films and wrote for more than 4000 nationally syndicated newspaper columns. He is known for saying, "I never met a man I didn't like." Rogers died in a plane crash with Wiley Post (American aviator who discovered the jet stream) in Point Barrow, Alaska.

Wog
A derogatory British term for a dark-skinned person from the Near or Middle East.

Ya Gazma
Egyptian curse calling for a shoe. Nothing is filthier than the bottom of a dirty shoe.

You're not done yet!

Read On For An Exciting Bonus Chapters

MURDER UNDER A BLACK MOON

ABIGAIL KEAM

Murder Under A Black Moon

A Mona Moon Mystery

Book 6

1

Mona entered the Moon box at Churchill Downs in order to watch the Kentucky Derby.

"Is she here—somewhere?" Aunt Melanie stammered, craning her neck around Mona. Before Mona could take her seat, Melanie pushed her aside to get a better look at the people milling behind them.

Flabbergasted, Mona hurriedly took a seat. "For goodness sake, Melanie. Get a hold of yourself. Mrs. Longworth is with Lord Farley checking the horses out in the paddock."

"I'm going to greet her."

Mona grabbed Melanie's arm. "Sit down, please. She'll be here shortly. Then you can talk her arm off."

"How did you manage to wrangle Alice

Roosevelt Longworth as a house guest?"

"I didn't. Lord Farley is her host. Apparently, the Roosevelts and Farleys are related. She wanted to come to the Derby and called Lord Farley up."

Melanie looked crestfallen. "You mean she's not staying at Moon Manor?"

"Afraid not. She's Lord Farley's guest."

"Quit referring to Robert as Lord Farley. We all know he is Lawrence Robert Emerton Dagobert Farley, Marquess of Gower," Melanie snapped. "And we all know you two are engaged. Stop rubbing it in."

Mona grinned. "It's eating you up, isn't it, Aunt Melanie?"

"You know it is. I had my cap set on Robert. Then my brother had the rude manners to make you his sole heir to the Moon fortune, and up and died on me before I could get the will changed. Without you butting in, I'm sure Robert would have fallen for me." Melanie straightened her hat. "I can't wait to see Manfred and give him a piece of my mind."

Mona studied her aunt to see if Melanie recognized the irony of her statement. Melanie would have to be dead in order to talk with her brother. It was a shame Melanie never saw the futility of her life. She was a lovely-looking woman with light eyes and blonde hair with pale ivory skin. She and Mona looked very much alike, but Mona's hair was platinum and her eyes a startling yellow—only two percent of the world's population had eyes the color of Mona's. They were near the same age as Melanie was the last bloom of her mother's womb. When Melanie was very small, Mona's father (Melanie's brother) married against his parent's wishes and left Moon Manor disinherited. But that's where the sameness ended as their temperaments were worlds apart.

Mona was a hard worker and college-educated, whereas Melanie whiled away her days lunching and gossiping with the "girls." Her education had been a Swiss finishing school that molded young women into potential helpmates for powerful men.

"You know that Alice and FDR aren't speaking because she supported Herbert Hoover running for president instead of her own cousin."

"Is that so?" Mona replied.

Melanie sniffed, "It's not the first public quarrel she's had. She supposedly buried a voodoo doll of William Howard Taft's daughter, Nellie, in the White House lawn after Taft won the presidency. Both the Taft and Wilson administrations banned her from the White House. I guess it will be only a matter of time before she does likewise with this administration."

"Bury an effigy of Mrs. Roosevelt in the White House lawn?" Mona teased.

"Ugh, Eleanor. I can't stand that high-pitched voice of hers—like nails squeaking on a chalkboard. Well, yes, I mean that Alice will do something that will get her banned from the White House again."

"And yet she is so popular."

"You know her father, Teddy Roosevelt—"

"I know who her father was, Melanie," Mona cut in.

Melanie continued unabashed, "Her father, President Theodore Roosevelt, said, 'I can be President of the United States, or I can control Alice. I cannot possibly do both.'"

Mona looked over her shoulder. Robert and Alice had been gone for a long time. She wondered what was holding them up. "Look at the crowd. Half the people are here to see the Derby and the other half to see Alice Roosevelt. I wonder who tipped the papers that she was coming."

"I have no idea," Melanie said nonchalantly, looking through her binoculars at the crowd.

Mona gave Melanie a hard look as she was suspicious of her aunt. Very few people knew Alice Roosevelt Longworth was coming, but there was always the possibility Miss Alice could have tipped off the papers herself.

Melanie leaned over and nudged Mona. "You know it is rumored Alice Roosevelt's daughter is not her husband's but sired by Senator William Borah."

"Who was sired by Senator Borah?" Willie Deatherage asked, entering the Moon private viewing box with a small tray of Mint Julep drinks and handed one to Mona and Melanie.

"Thank you, dear," Mona said. "Very thoughtful of you."

Melanie said, "I so love this drink. Wouldn't be Derby Day without a Mint Julep." Seeing Willie's stricken face, Melanie added, "Oh, sorry,

Willie. I forgot that you are on the wagon."

Willie took her seat and ignored Melanie's snide remark. She made it a habit long ago to pay little attention to the woman.

Dexter Deatherage, his hands full of drinks also, stumbled into the box. "Here, someone help me before I drop these. I got extras because I don't want to be running up and down the aisles for refreshments."

Mona and Willie reached over and relieved Dexter of his burden.

"Who are we talking about now?" Dexter asked, handing his wife a cold Coca Cola bottle from his pocket and a ginger ale from his other pocket.

"I was saying that it is rumored that Paulina Longworth is not the child of Nicholas Longworth, but Senator William Borah," Melanie said.

"This is unseemly talk," Mona admonished. "Gossip like this can ruin a woman."

Ignoring Mona, Willie said, "I heard she wanted to name the baby Deborah. Get it—de Borah. The family nicknamed the child Aurora Borah Alice."

Dexter suggested, "Ladies, quit talking about

our distinguished guest like that. It is scandalous."

"Oh, Dexter, you're such a stick-in-the-mud," Willie complained about her husband.

"Be that as it may, my dearest, let's show some decorum. Robert and Alice will be here any moment. I passed them on the way."

Mona asked, "What's taking them so long?"

"Mrs. Longworth is being bombarded by the crowds wanting her autograph or presenting her with Teddy bears. They're making their way through slowly."

"Aren't the Pinkertons keeping the crowds away?" Mona asked, perturbed. The last thing she wanted was for Alice Roosevelt Longworth, daughter of a popular dead U.S. President to be harmed on her watch.

Dexter answered, "It seems Mrs. Longworth is having a grand time meeting her devoted public. The Pinkertons are helpless but to obey her commands."

Mona sighed in relief until she heard sharp voices rise from the spectator box next to theirs as a young man and woman were arguing. "Melanie, let me see those binoculars."

Melanie swung the binoculars over to the couple.

"What are they saying?" Willie asked.

"They are arguing over another woman," Melanie said.

An older couple tried to quiet them down. Finally, the young woman burst into tears and rushed out of the box. The middle-aged couple and the young man looked astonished. The young man started to rush after the fleeing woman, but the older woman pulled him back and coaxed him into his seat.

Mona assumed the older couple were the young man's parents. Grabbing the binoculars from Melanie, she said, "Give back my binoculars. I wish you'd buy your own."

"I would if you upped my pitiful stipend."

"Oh, stop with that. You make more money in a year than ninety-nine percent of the country."

"You can never be too rich or too thin," Melanie replied.

"Who are they?" Mona asked.

Melanie scrunched her nose and said, "They are Jeannie and Zeke Duff. New money. Oil wells from somewhere west of the Pecos I expect. The young chap in the seersucker suit is their son Cody."

Willie shot Melanie a disdainful look. "They are oil people from Texas. They had black gold on their land and cashed in. They have relocated here and are itching to break into the horse business."

"Good luck to them," Melanie said, ruefully. "They are nothing but social climbers as far as I'm concerned. The last thing the Bluegrass needs is more parvenus."

Willie rolled her eyes.

"And the young woman?" Mona asked.

Willie added, "The tearful woman is his new bride, Helen."

Dexter added, "From Texas as well."

Willie said, "I hear they are having a difficult time blending in, especially the new wife. She wants to go back to Texas."

"I can attest to how difficult it is to make friends here if one is new," Mona said.

"I resent that," Willie teased.

"I don't mean you and Dexter, of course, but born and bred Lexingtonians are very snobbish.

You must admit that, Willie."

"We don't like to see new money come in and buy up our land," Willie said.

Dexter argued, "But, darling, the old aristocrats don't have the money to hang on to these farms. They are expensive to run. The Depression has hit everyone. Look at John Keene. He wants to sell his farm for Lexington's new racecourse, and his family has been here since the 1700s."

"Well, the Wrights didn't do so badly buying land for Calumet Farm," Melanie concurred. "Old man Wright saved the land from the bulldozer."

Willie mused, "I wonder how it's going with the son changing it from a Standardbred horse farm to a Thoroughbred horse farm. Big difference in training."

"I saw Warren Wright the other day. He said things were going fine at Calumet Farm, and he hopes to have a champion soon," Mona said.

"Don't hold your breath," Melanie scoffed. "He's got nothing but plugs at the moment."

"I'm not sure I would agree, Melanie," Dexter said. "Warren Wright is a sharp cookie."

Melanie harrumphed.

"Who are the other couples in their box?" Willie asked.

Melanie strained her neck in order to get a good gander. "The woman in the red dress and big Derby hat is Natasha Merriweather and her husband Tosh. She is the daughter of an iron magnate and, like the Duffs, wants to learn the racing business. They recently bought Pennygate Farm."

Mona nodded. "I had heard Pennygate had been sold."

"Well, they bought it," Willie added.

"And the other couple?" Mona asked.

Melanie stood and twisted toward their neighboring box, waving to some friends who had yoo-hooed her. Sitting back down, she said, "That's Rusty Thompson and his wife. He's a trainer and buyer for folks who have cash to burn."

"Was," Dexter said.

Mona turned to watch Dexter take a sip of his Mint Julep. "What do you mean by 'was?'"

Willie fanned herself with a racing program. "Mona, don't you know anything that's going on in town?"

Mona laughed, "I've been preoccupied."

"Did you say you've been preoccupied, darling? I hope it's because you've been planning our wedding."

Mona looked up and smiled. There Robert was—the light of her life.

Robert escorted a distinguished looking woman wearing a blue chiffon day dress into the Moon spectator box. "Everyone, I'd like you to meet my guest, Mrs. Nicholas Longworth."

Everyone in the box stood in greeting as did everyone around them who was eavesdropping.

Mrs. Longworth took her program and patted Robert on the chest with it. "Dear boy, always introduce a woman by her own name. I hate that ancient practice of introducing a woman by her husband's name, especially if he's deceased. Rather Edwardian, don't you think?"

Grinning, Robert gave a small bow. "Excusez-moi, Madame. May I present Alice Roosevelt Longworth."

"I found the name of Alice Roosevelt gets me in the better addresses rather than Longworth, and I only refer to my dead husband's name when I need money from the bank."

Everyone twittered.

Mona felt Willie give her a small nudge as if to say "I told you so."

Robert helped Alice to her seat and took the one next to her before introducing everyone.

Alice gave the once-over to Melanie and Mona. "You girls sure stick out with your hair color. Are you sisters?"

"I am Melanie Moon, Miss Alice."

"I got that in the introduction."

"Mona is my niece."

Alice gave Mona a long hard stare. "So, you are the cartographer who runs Moon Enterprises. Everyone is losing their shirts, but Moon Enterprises is having a profitable year and employing more men. My hat off to you, young woman."

"Thank you, Miss Alice. High praise coming from you."

"I think of such people as yourself as the real key to getting this country back on its feet rather than my cousin's ridiculous federal programs. People need to rely on themselves and not the government to get them out of a jam."

"I find that people who hold such beliefs are

people with lots of money at their disposal," Mona countered.

Willie murmured, "Oh boy, here we go." She gulped down some ginger ale, knowing of Mona's strong support for FDR's New Deal programs and Alice's dislike of them.

Melanie interjected, "I think what my niece means is—"

Alice cut in, "I know exactly what your niece means. You interested in politics, Miss Moon?"

"Not really, but I help those less fortunate where I can, but call me Mona, please."

"I shall."

Mona leaned forward. "You and I agree on this, Miss Alice—it's jobs that are going to turn this country around. Putting men back to work. The unemployment rate is still twenty-one percent."

Alice asked, "You interested in politics, Melanie?"

Melanie scoffed, "Hardly."

"I'm surprised."

"Why is that?"

"Because politics is a blood sport, and I think you might be pretty good at blood sports."

"Thank you, Miss Alice," Melanie replied in a small voice. She wasn't sure if she had just been insulted or praised.

"Enough of this bantering," Robert said. "The race is getting ready to start."

Everyone stood to sing the Kentucky Derby anthem—My Old Kentucky Home. After the song, there was a crowd murmur as the Derby horses pranced onto the racetrack. Once all horses were placed in the starting gate, a bell rang and they were off with the crowd rushing onto the track itself and running behind the horses.

AND THEY'RE OFF! Peace Chance and Mata Hari speed off with Mata Hari stepping into the lead. Turning in front of the stand with the mob screaming loudly, Mata Hari is in the lead at three comfortable lengths with Quasimodo second and Speedmore third. On the backstretch, it's Mata Hari opening up with Sgt. Byrne now head to head. At the mile post, it's Sgt. Byrne now in front with Mata Hari second. Cavalcade now coming up and challenging both Sgt. Bryne and Mata Hari. Heading home, it's Cavalcade on the outside with Discovery shooting ahead. Cavalcade and Discovery fighting it out as Mata Hari and Sgt. Byrne fade. Two hundred yards to go, it's Discovery in front and here comes Cavalcade fighting for the roses. They are neck to neck with Cavalcade not giving up. Cavalcade is too much for Discovery. Cavalcade can't be stopped, and it's Cavalcade two and a half lengths ahead. Cavalcade wins the sixtieth run of the Kentucky Derby! Discovery is second and Agrarian comes in third!

Robert tore up his ticket. "That does it. I bet on Mata Hari. She just gave out."

"I told you to bet on Cavalcade. Look at his wide chest. Lungs are what wins these races," Alice said, looking smug and holding up her ticket. "I'm going to cash mine in."

A piercing scream rang out over the noise of the crowd, causing everyone to search for the source.

Mona stood. "I don't think that scream sounded like someone who has the winning ticket."

"Or they lost the winning ticket," Willie said.

The scream sounded again and continued into

a low mournful hum. Another woman started screaming and sobbing.

"It's coming from the next box!" Mona said.

Everyone in the next box was huddled around a man slumped over in his seat.

"What happened? Do you need help?" Dexter called out as he climbed over the rail that divided the review boxes.

Mona and Robert followed Dexter into the next box.

"Do you need a doctor?" Mona asked a pale and sweating Zeke Duff.

Duff replied, "No, I'm afraid we need the police!" He pointed to the man slumped over.

Mona went over to feel for a pulse when Dexter grabbed her hand. "Don't touch him, Mona. He is beyond your ministrations."

Mona looked closer and noticed small drops of blood trickling down the man's shirt and tie. It was then she realized the unfortunate man was truly dead and caught the sight of the gruesome cause.

The victim had a woman's hat pin protruding from his bloodied left eye!

About The Author

Hi. I'm Abigail Keam. I write the best-selling *Josiah Reynolds Mystery Series* and the *Mona Moon Mystery Series*. I also write *The Princess Maura Tales* (Epic Fantasy) and the *Last Chance For Love Romance Series* (Sweet Romance novellas).

Like my protagonist Josiah Reynolds, I am a professional beekeeper and have won sixteen awards from the Kentucky State Fair. I live in a metal house with my husband and various critters on a cliff overlooking the Kentucky River.

If you like my stories, please leave a review at place of purchase. For the latest new and fun tidbits – follow me on my FB Author's Page. I always love to hear from my readers. I would love to hear from you!